Justice 4.1

The Tsarina Sector
Book I

By

Jim Webster

Safkhet Publishing

First published in 2014 by Safkhet Fantasy, London, United Kingdom
Safkhet Fantasy is an imprint of Safkhet Publishing
www.safkhetpublishing.com

1

ISBN 978-1-908208-23-1

Printed and bound by Lightning Source International

Typeset in Crimson and Neuropolitical

Find out more about Jim on jandbvwebster.wordpress.com
or on Facebook at www.facebook.com/TsarinaSector

Author Jim Webster
Copy Editor Jamie Davidson
Cover Designer Sally Neuhaus
Managing Editor William Banks Sutton
Proofreader Walter Richardson

The colophon of Safkhet is a representation of the ancient Egyptian goddess of wisdom and knowledge, who is credited with inventing writing.
Safkhet Publishing is named after her because the founders met in Egypt.

Dedication

To Brenda, Katharine, Sheila and Clare.

Because they're worth it.

The Cast

Tsarina Sector Government

Haldar Drom......................Head of Investigative Services
Inspector Bartan Galway..Police Officer, New Charity Gendarmerie
Toulis Hart.........................Insurance loss adjuster, Trans-world Insurance.
Willon Cartif......................Broadcaster, Tsarina Broadcasting, Channel Six
Vladimir Kaunas ....Hereditary Governor of Tsarina
Doran Stilan.......................Head of the Diplomatic Service of Tsarina

The Serendipity

Shilla..................................Captain
Tongo.................................First mate, cook
Fingle.................................The first engineer
Harper ....The second engineer
Lallan.................................Professional gambler and relief cook.
Patti...................................Cargo loader and paramedic
Wingo ....Ex-Navy weapons-tech, and handles the light laser turret, all the electrics and navigational systems
Zenobia ....Second cargo loader, nurse and child care specialist

Tsarina Marines

Colonel Aled ....Commander of the Marine Regiment
Captain Gillik ....Commander, Reaction Company
Jonno.................................Marine rapid deployment Battalion commander
Captain Aldor Issil ....Captain of the Taurus
Sergeant Lian Gorfan........Electronic warfare technician

The Crime Lord

Wayland Strang.................Rumoured to be The Starmancer

Chapter 1

The flitter was hardly luxurious. It was a spacious workhorse with just enough concessions to comfort to deter personal injury claims from those who hired it. At the moment, it loitered over the northern highlands of the Border Kingdoms at a safe altitude. To their north, the highlands rose steadily until they became snow-capped and were lost in the clouds. Below them was a jumbled badlands of gorges and ridges, twisted rock, frost-shattered and crumbling. Wheeling below them was a pair of great four-winged aradons, keen-eyed carrion feeders. In the distance, perhaps five miles away, Kilonwin Kardoverin could just make out what might be another pair. As far as he could tell, they were the only signs of life in sight. He looked down; even with vision enhancers, the ridges showed virtually no sign of life. He counted three stunted bushes with occasional blades of grass poking through the loose scree.

Kardoverin strapped himself into the co-pilot seat and fiddled with the camera array, determined to get as much footage as possible. Kardoverin had a reputation in the industry as one of the best documentary makers in the sector. This reputation was based on arrogance, a casual disregard for personal safety, and painstaking camera work. He was reputed to get five times as much material as was needed, even for top quality holo work. He turned to the pilot. "Can we get lower? I'd like to film into those gorges."

"Why?"

"Well, there's damn all up here."

"Why not zoom?" The pilot sounded nervous.

"They're in heavy shadow."

"Look, this is the Border Kingdoms, it isn't safe."

Kardoverin adjusted the central rig and raked the peripheral arrays so that they covered both flanks.

"Take us down fast; we'll be through and out."

"They're barbarians! They shoot at people."

"With black powder weapons." Kardoverin's tone was dismissive as he checked the satellite relay. It seemed to be working perfectly. "Look, just go in, one quick fly-through. It isn't as if I'm asking you to land, or even hover."

The pilot muttered something blasphemous under his breath and brought the flitter round. "I'll take us up that gorge on the left, it's narrower. Being so overcast, it's less likely to be inhabited."

He opened the throttle and brought the bow of the flitter sharply down. The clumsy craft accelerated rather faster than Kardoverin had expected, and he hastily checked the camera focus. This model of vehicle was effectively a rectangular box which flew and had little consideration of style. But for his purposes, the open top meant it had been comparatively easy to fit the cameras. The pilot brought them down sharply, heading south, gaining speed as he lost altitude. Then suddenly, he spun the controls and the flitter turned and banked so sharply Kardoverin felt himself hanging in the harness. Then the pilot pointed the nose of his craft straight into the mouth of the gorge, still dropping and gaining speed. As they entered between the towering rock walls, they were barely twenty feet above the ground and moving faster than Kardoverin would have believed possible. Kardoverin kept his eyes on the monitors, running his fingers over the controls in front of him, altering the zoom, the angle, the filters. They were deep in the gorge now and the boxy craft was travelling at breakneck speed. Kardoverin constantly re-adjusted the controls. "Isn't this a bit fast?"

The pilot's answer came through clenched teeth. "If I could go faster, I would. I want us out of here and—" He paused. "Oh hell, we are in deep—"

There was a staccato rattle of automatic weapons fire from one side. The burst struck the pilot, jerking his body against the seat harness. Kardoverin tore his gaze from the monitors and looked towards where the noise had come from. The second burst hit the front of the flitter, and the engine began to whine. Kardoverin frantically unbuckled his harness and stood up to reach over the pilot's body for the controls. The third burst struck him in the chest, spun him round and left him draped over the side of the flitter. Thirty seconds later, with no one at the controls, the flitter struck the rock wall of the gorge and exploded.

*****

Haldar Drom, Head of Investigative Services, Governor's Investigation Office, settled back in his chair as the lights dimmed and two techs fiddled with the settings on the hologram. The opening credits rolled, accompanied by music Haldar was sure he'd heard played in a lift somewhere. As the techs fiddled, the holo expanded to fill a third of the room; apparently satisfied, they moved back to their chairs at either end of the semicircle.

The holo started with a schematic of the galaxy, viewed from the traditional starting point of Man, old Earth herself. The view panned across the galaxy before zooming in to the galactic rim, still viewed from somewhere nearer to the galactic centre.

The voice-over started. "I was told at school that *somewhere* has to be the edge of the galaxy, and in this program, we take you there." The holo zoomed through the schematic at speed, leaving some of those watching suffering from a vague sense of vertigo. The apparent motion became more sedate: the viewpoint, moving further and further out, to the wisp of stars on the galaxy's outer fringes. "And here is Wilbur's Wisp, and here (as the holo zoomed in) is the star at the furthermost edge of the Wisp. This is a star so insignificant that even the locals still call it by its catalogue number, MM43-62." The holo continued to zoom in, "and here is Tsarina, quite literally the edge of our universe."

Haldar prodded the man in the next chair, Guthan Teel, Head of Technology in the Governor's Investigation Office. "I thought they got permission to film because it would be a boost to trade and tourism."

"You should see the stuff some of their competitors have produced in the past," Guthan replied, sardonically. "These people are positively gushing compared to the others." He gestured to the holo. "They had to be, considering the amount of our stock footage they scrounged."

The holo now showed Tsarina rotating in the centre, while various minor figures appeared around it, strutted briefly as the voice-over mentioned them, and then disappeared.

"Savants tell us that Tsarina wasn't as much colonized as infected by humanity—explored for the sake of completeness and named after the exploration ship's purser's dog." An improbable dog borrowed from a children's cartoon frolicked across the picture. "Ignored for generations, Tsarina achieved brief fame under the Salid Emperors. Salin IV was something of an astronomer and planned to build an observatory on the planet. When he died at the hands of the usurper Salin V, also known as Salin the Paranoid, the new emperor visited Tsarina to try and work out what his predecessor had really been planning. He decided that Tsarina would be a useful defence post in the case of invasion from the globular clusters that orbit the galaxy. I suppose that just goes to show how paranoid he was. He appointed a military governor, but to prevent the new officer plotting to overthrow him, there was no budget to go with the role."

Guthan leaned across to Haldar as a succession of ancient likenesses passed through the holo. "Nothing much changes, then."

"Given that you take a good three quarters of the Investigation Office budget, that's a bit rich."

Guthan grinned at him. "In our hands, it's invested; we are the one part of government that runs at a profit. You just blow it on salaries and fripperies like that."

The voice-over continued, oblivious to their comments. "The original military governor was a man of infinite resource, with contacts in the prison service. He 'conscripted' both long-term prisoners and those condemned to death. By calling them the garrison, he managed to ship them to Tsarina using ships of the Imperial Navy thus securing, at minimal cost, the permanent defensive capabilities of the outpost. Yet, it was the fourth hereditary governor, Kaunas, who was the first to actually visit the planet. He had enemies in Court, including the entire Imperial family. Hence, Kaunas fled to Tsarina with just a few friends, a couple of ships, and a full rebel Marine Division."

"You can see why he numbered the Imperial family among his enemies,"

Guthan grunted. "Not sure why we're getting the history lesson, though."

"It gives the viewer context, and allows the series' writers to claim their stuff is educational—and that entitles them to ransack the various communities' school budgets." Haldar pondered briefly, "Which is something we haven't tried ourselves yet."

The holo viewpoint had zoomed in much closer to the planet and was picking out details of geography. It showed Kaunas City, situated on the extreme western end of the continent of Lorenz. There were some shots of the delta at the mouth of the Colitas River, picturesque moss-shrouded tree stumps overshadowing small channels, inter-cut with stock footage of wildlife. The view passed up the river, pointing out the towns and giving various details and views taken at street level. There was Warren, built on stilts above a plain infested by giant gastropods reared for their meat and mucus trails; Lydia, the town built over a lake, myriad walkways snaking between impractically ornate stilt houses, floating islands and houseboats; and Kenehan, where the forest and town are intertwined, and where the finest furniture in the galaxy is made. The holo then moved back to Kaunas City and along the coast to overlook the straits of Farrant, which separates Lorenz from Akin. The holo showed the sea-scoured rocks of the straits, small indigenous amphibious creatures scrambled about on sucker-tipped feet, searching the scarlet weed for invertebrates. The sound of the roaring water forced through the tidal narrows reverberated around the room. The viewpoint pulled out and the noise lessened to allow the voice-over to continue.

"But for this program we are going to concentrate on the exotic inhabitants of Akin, especially the mountain principalities which border the lands settled by the 'Church of the Numinous Atmosphere'. This bizarre sect has, for many generations, comprehensively failed to maintain order among its neighbours." There were groans from around the semicircle and one voice, Rolor's, said, "We'll sue!" There was laugher round the room; Rolor, one of the department's design engineers, came from Akin.

Another voice spoke up. It was Doran Stilan, head of the diplomatic service. "Do we need the full program? Can we not just cut to the interesting bit?"

"Not like you to want us to skip the pretty girls, Doran."

Haldar recognized the voice; it was the Governor, Vladimir Kaunas. He must have wandered in late; Haldar had not seen him arrive.

"You know me, Vladimir, but given the age of this stock footage, they'll probably be grandmothers by now."

Haldar felt he ought to keep the meeting focused. "Guthan, please have your techs take us to just before the incident. I'll get up and talk us through it."

Haldar stood up and unconsciously straightened his suit jacket. Too long in uniform, he always felt half-dressed in civilian clothes. He walked to the low lectern by the Hologram. The tech pointed to a keypad on the lectern and gave him whispered instructions as to how the keys worked. There were times when he wished Guthan and his staff could just stop 'improving' everything. He took a quick look at the hologram and saw it was ready. He pressed the play button.

"This footage was shot at the end, it was never edited, has no voice-over and isn't part of any broadcast, but we got it when we intercepted everything else. Now if you look here," Haldar gestured with the pointer, "you will see the sides of the gorge as the flitter enters. The camera work is excellent, the detail as good as one could hope for. We see an empty gorge, with a stream running at the bottom. This is pretty much what we'd expect in such an infertile area; grass of sorts growing through shattered lichen-covered rock, even a yak cow suckling a calf. Just the sort of thing the camera man was probably looking for. There's even a few more yak being herded by children wearing yak-hide clothing, perfect for local colour. But now look," Haldar froze the scene. "We're further into the gorge. Strangely, the gorge floor has been cleared of fallen rock; indeed it has been levelled." He moved the pointer. "Down this face, we can see someone has gone to the trouble of cutting a road. And here, look, we can see a column of people on the road, most of them in shapeless smocks." He played with the zoom and the people filled the image. "As you can see, virtually all the people appear to be female, wearing what I would describe as surgical gowns." He moved the pointer along the line. "This figure here is also carrying what looks like a firearm. The locals are allowed only such as they can produce themselves, normally traditional single-shot weapons which use homemade black powder."

Haldar zoomed out and allowed the film to continue. "As you can see there are further parties. Some appear to be porters carrying quite large loads, here, here, here and especially here." His pointer stabbed out in time with his words. "And at this point, things are starting to go badly wrong. From the change in camera angles, we can see the craft is starting to climb. I suspect the pilot has seen something, and I suspect it was..." Haldar paused, allowed the film to run, and then froze it, "This."

In the centre of the holo was the figure of a man. He was dressed in heavy, shapeless winter clothing, but the freeze frame had caught him in the act of bringing a weapon to bear. Haldar continued "Here we see something that should not be present. No black-powder weapon, this." He zoomed in. The figure grew until it filled the holo but was starting to lose focus. "I suspect that this is a reasonably modern combat rifle." Haldar allowed the sequence to run, and the blurred figure could be seen to work a bolt on the weapon to cock it, and then bring it to his shoulder. As the audience watched in silence, the rifleman fired three bursts; seconds later, the holo lost focus, flashed white, and stopped. "You might have noticed," Haldar added, "that there was no sign of cartridges being ejected. This weapon is using caseless ammunition."

"I'd say he was using an Altech Defender." The voice was that of Doran Stilan. "We use them in Embassy Protection; they're a decent rifle. Altech manufacture them on at least six worlds in the Wisp and far more beyond, so they're good to get spare parts for. Trouble is they're so widespread they're virtually generic, but the least I can do is have my people check our inventory, see if there are any missing."

"If you will, Doran," said Governor Vladimir from his seat behind everyone else. "We've spent a lot of time keeping effective military technology out of the hands of the Border Kingdoms. I don't want to see that hard work wasted because someone in stores gets greedy."

Vladimir got to his feet and made his way out to the front. "I hope I don't have to tell you gentlemen and ladies that this information is not to go any further. A rifle out of place is not a cause for panic. I certainly don't want various authorities on Akin getting upset. I've already had an urgent request for a meeting from the Patriarch of the Church of the Numinous Atmosphere." Vladimir turned to Haldar. "And how long have we had a policy of reconnaissance by journalist?"

Haldar pondered his words. "Formally, never, but in reality, given budgetary constraints, it is a cost effective way of monitoring the periphery."

"Put like that, I'm probably in favour." Vladimir turned to those sitting listening to him. "So Doran, can you get back to me and to Haldar here quickly?"

The head of the diplomatic service twitched the cuffs of his Watch Company dress uniform. "I can give him details of stocks on Tsarina tomorrow at the latest, but obviously stocks off-world in embassies will take weeks to come in."

"Right, Haldar, you provide me with an assessment of the situation once you've got the details from Doran and his department."

Haldar gathered his notes from the lectern. "That we will do, Sir."

*****

When Haldar walked out of the meeting, Guthan accompanied him. "Guthan, can you get me full location details of the incident? I would like a chance to take a look before too many people start to remove the evidence."

"Easily done; but aren't you waiting for the report from the Embassy Protection?"

"Forward it to me. I want to get out into the Border Kingdoms and see what's going on."

"In person?"

Haldar said ruefully, "due to the fact that we've not got any budget left to fritter away on field agents, yes." They walked a little way down the corridor and he added, "At the moment, I have three full-time field agents and a dozen more who hold down steady jobs working for other people but report to me. So I'm going to have to go myself."

They reached the door that led to the wing housing the Governor's Investigation Office. Haldar opened the door and allowed Guthan through first. Guthan paused. "Before you go, there is someone you will have to meet. We have an Inspector Galway of the New Charity Gendarmerie who has arrived on official business."

"Do we have any relations with New Charity? I'm a bit vague as to where it is."

"I had to look it up; they're a rather prosperous agricultural world not too far from Havadon, at the foot of Wilbur's Wisp. Obviously with Havadon being a major trading and manufacturing world with limited agricultural resources, New Charity does pretty well out of the deal. But back to your point, their police are recognized as at least adequate in all the local sector and sub-sector policing agreements and they're signatories of the Wilbur's Wisp co-responsibility agreement. So he's unlikely to be a torturer, and he probably isn't corrupt."

"OK, I might as well see him now; get it out of the way. But why does he want me?"

Guthan stopped by the office door. "You forget, we don't have a planet-wide policing authority, because..." and here he paused as if recollecting a quote. "*We're a proud collection of autonomous and self-governing communities.*

Hence, off-planet bodies always talk to the Governor's Office. In this case, that means you."

"Up until now, I've avoided dealing with the rest of the universe. I've enough problems at home. Have him join me in the dining room, since it's about time to eat. Anything else?"

Guthan thought briefly. "Could you sweet-talk the Marines for me? I've had a call from SRCC, they want an electronic warfare officer up on the satellite promptly, and the Marines owe you more favours than they owe me."

Haldar sounded genuinely surprised. "I thought you were always giving the Marines new toys to play with before you sold them to everyone else."

"Problem is," here Guthan sounded embarrassed, "they expect experimental kit to work all the time and get upset when it malfunctions. They're not the ideal test subjects. But at least they don't actually charge me for testing them."

*****

Sergeant Lian Gorfan propelled himself along the line that stretched between the shuttle and satellite base station. When he was a child, his grandmother had always said, disparagingly, 'that lad don't know which way's up!' Well, now he did. Forget about the universe, up is defined by the airlock you are leaving.

Another thing he'd learned in the marines, quality was shown in little things. It was the care taken by the tech who serviced your vac suit, the care taken when 'throwing the line' between two vessels; or in this case the care the shuttle pilot had taken to align the shuttle airlock with the base station airlock so both were the 'same way up'. Indeed the SRCC team which had placed the base station in orbit had made sure that its 'top' was aligned with the north pole of Tsarina. It seems a little thing, but it meant that as he moved along the line, he didn't have a vertiginous feeling that he was about to plunge a thousand miles down to the planet surface. No, the planet was hanging there ahead of him, just to the left of the base station.

He glided along the line, the momentum of his first jump carrying him smoothly along. Ahead of him, it must have been early afternoon in Kaunas City; he couldn't make out the city itself but could see the straits of Farrant. Akin was moving through evening, great swirls of dark cloud covered it, thickening toward the north.

He turned his attention to the station ahead of him. The hull plates were enamelled, another useful indicator that someone was taking care. The enamel coating wore better than steel, and if you expected the installation to last into its second century, enamelling was a cost-effective process. He reached the airlock, swung down, punched the 'open' button and waited for the door to slide open.

He unclipped from the line and stepped into the airlock. He put down his tool chest and stood at ease, glancing around while waiting for the air pressure to equalise. Above the internal door, moulded into the metal was the slogan, "The Sands River Citrus Cooperative: Serving its members for over four thousand four hundred years." Lian had read up about the SRCC in the shuttle. Formed initially as an agricultural cooperative it had branched out into meteorological prediction and weather satellites. From there to providing 'intra-system traffic control services' was a small step. Now the SRCC had a presence in well over a thousand systems, and insurance premiums were lower if you were shipping in an SRCC-monitored system.

The inner door of the airlock opened, and Lian could see two men waiting for him, each wearing nondescript grey overalls with SRCC badges on the left breast. Lian unfastened his helmet. "Good day, gentlemen. I am Sergeant Lian Gorfan of Tsarina Marine Division; I believe you have a problem."

The older of the two men stepped forward. His head was shaven and tattooed extensively, Lian put him down as a Hubwards Initiate from Kraft.

"I'm Taf, the Meteorologist," said the man. "This is Aran, my colleague and intra-system traffic controller. I'll try and explain while you take your vac suit off." Lian gave him a casual salute and nodded to Aran. Aran too, had his head shaved, but Lian noticed that his overalls were short-sleeved and that on his arms and hands sections of the skin appeared to be covered with small mirrors. These mirrors were flexible; Lian noticed that they conformed to the movements of the skin.

Lian started to remove his gloves. Taf, with the air of a lecturer faced with students of uncertain intellect, began. "What do you know about computers?"

Lian looked up from unfastening the seals on his torso plate. "Well, I hold the standard naval qualifications."

"So you know that no one in their right mind links one computer to another so they can communicate electronically."

Lian parroted the answer from one of his training manuals. "This is Standard Operating Procedure to stop some bright twelve year old producing a virus which can disrupt banking systems or send power stations off-line."

"Exactly," Taf sounded like he was trying to encourage one of the slower members of class, "and so we communicate with computers through a keyboard, voice, hand-signals or by having them use optical recognition software on printed documents. Except that, at SRCC, we don't. Because of the sheer volume of meteorological data, we have to use electronic transfer as well."

Lian felt he had to prove he wasn't out of his depth here so interjected, "Some warships use linked systems as well, but obviously they are sealed from outside contact."

Taf smiled in a slightly patronising manner. "And obviously we make sure that software is securely hardwired into the computer. This reduces the risk of problems introduced from outside."

Lian had finally taken his vac suit off and hung it on the peg next to the airlock. Aran, who had been listening to the conversation with a slightly amused expression said, "You both ignore the fact that deeper towards the galactic core they allow computers to communicate electronically as standard. It's just we haven't the sophistication to cope with either their viruses or their informal attempts to take over our systems." He rubbed his eyes with one hand and added, "I suggest we just show him the problem."

"OK. I just didn't want our systems here to come as a surprise to him." Taf sounded a little hurt.

"I *am* an electronic warfare technician," Lian said, slightly put out by their attitude, "I'm only ever surprised by systems that are properly maintained and doing what they were designed to do."

Aran beckoned Lian to follow, and he stepped through a hatch into the control room. This room had two chairs, each facing a bank of computers.

"This is where we work; above is the living area," Aran explained.

"If you can call a sleeping space the size of a coffin a bedroom, and an exercise bike mounted above the galley table a gym, then we lack for nothing," Taf muttered.

Aran sat at one of the chairs. He raised a hand above his head and spoke briskly in a language Lian didn't know. Four screens seemed to be extruded from the walls, each as tall as he was, and broader than they were tall. Aran gave another command, and the screens came to life. The big wall screen above him showed a section of space with Tsarina placed centre-stage. "We default to screens rather than holo, as that allows us to work on different projects at the same time," Aran said. He raised his other hand and then brought both hands down by his sides. The screen dimmed, and instead Tsarina hung in the middle of the room. Round it orbited moons, satellites and various half-remembered pieces of debris. "This is the view that started it all. It's footage that we stored when we decided it might be useful."

Taf seamlessly cut across him. "I was using it for visual meteorological confirmation of our predictions."

"It's the equivalent of looking out of the window to check," Aran added helpfully. "Anyway, as he was watching this, I saw a jump flash in the top far corner; it'll be coming along any moment." As they watched, the distinctive jump flash, which you get whenever a ship drops out of hyperspace, appeared, faded and was gone. "Someone had entered the system, so I routinely logged into the intra-system traffic system, and waited for whoever it was to contact us with their flight plan. Nothing happened." Aran glanced across to Lian. "This isn't that uncommon, some ships' crews are slow, some forget, some are a bit casual, and some are smugglers or similar." He pointed to another screen and said something in the same sing-song language. The screen became live, this one showing columns of numbers. "So I went into the data to find the ship, get a bearing on it and then contact them. But there was no ship."

Lian felt he ought to contribute something. "Is that common?"

"Well, is shouldn't be, but is," Aran admitted. "There are six geostationary satellites which collect data and beam it to us, using each other as relays, so you can get a lag. But after five minutes I got a little concerned, so I queried the appropriate satellite and took another dump of raw data." He gestured and a long column of figures appeared on the screen. "This I analysed by eye on the screen, and I noticed this." Aran gestured at the screen with a rod that had been clipped to his seat. The row of numbers he pointed at flashed red. "This is a ship entering; the line gives time, transponder code, heading, acceleration, velocity." Aran gave a command, "and this is the information I was getting from this computer." A second column of figures appeared, next to the first. "As you can see this ship has been totally ignored."

"How does that happen?" Lian asked.

"In theory, it cannot happen. So I went back through all original data and did a check to see if this ship had ever been seen before. It had been picked up by the satellites, its details had been transmitted to us, but it had never been picked up in the processed data."

"So what do you think is happening?"

Aran glanced at Taf. "Well, we put our heads together. We came to the conclusion that somewhere in this station there was a problem. I went through the various components and decided it would have to be the processor that accepts the data from all the relays and analyses it to produce the big picture." Aran clapped his hands and spoke. The hologram changed. "You are now looking at a 'real-time' view of the system, showing Tsarina in the centre, a ring of satellites around it marked as little red jewels, and various symbols for various ships moving slowly across the screen. The ship whose jump flash we saw won't show in this. We have played it forward and back for all the times we know the ship entered the system, and it has never appeared."

Lian studied the screen. "So which processor is it?"

Aran gestured with a foot. "It's this one down here. Take the cover off and you will see there are six boards. Tell us what you think."

II

Lian knelt down and, pulling a screwdriver from his tool belt, unscrewed the cover. He laid the cover to one side and examined the boards suspiciously.

"Were they all put in at the same time?"

"According to the records, these are the boards put in together some forty years ago, so they're all the same age," said Taf.

"Then why is this one a slightly darker shade than the others?"

"My guess is that it is from a different production batch. But according to the records, they're all the same batch, installed on the same day."

"I'll get my toolbox." Lian stepped out of the control centre and returned a minute later trundling the box behind him on its wheels. "Do you mind if I take a look?"

Aran glanced at Taf and said, "Be our guest; that is why we asked for help."

Lian opened one of the drawers in his toolbox and rooted through it, finally producing an optical probe. "Can I plug it directly into a screen?"

Taf took the cable and plugged it into a socket; immediately they saw displayed a probe's-eye view. Lian knelt down by the open processor case. He swiftly snapped together the stand so that the probe was supported. He then adjusted the stand so that the probe would pass above the boards without touching anything. Then he stood up and stepped back. He gestured to the pad in his hand. "With this control I can have my device move forward without making physical contact with the processor."

The three men watched the screen as the mechanism moved slowly forward. It passed along the length of the suspect board until Lian halted it. "Now I'll try various wavelengths." On the screen the probe remained still, but the illumination varied as it blocked out different wavelengths. Suddenly the screen had a faint red glow.

"Infra-red, interesting." Lian continued to allow the apparatus to check other wavelengths, but eventually brought it back to Infra-red. Slowly the probe eased forward again. At the far edge of the board Lian stopped the probe and gestured at the screen.

"You don't see many of these. Can you see that very narrow beam of infra-red?" The other two nodded, fascinated. "Well, your board takes very slightly more current than it should, and uses the extra to produce that beam." Lian altered the probe angle carefully. "And there you can see the receptor, equally small. The whole set up is to catch a beam less than a mil across."

"So what is it doing?" Taf asked.

"Think of it as a tripwire. Break the beam, or move the board so that the beam no longer hits the receptor, and something will happen."

"What?" Aran sounded more intrigued than nervous.

"A good question." Lian started the probe moving forward even more slowly. "But it tends not to be good, otherwise the manufacturer would have mentioned it." Lian halted the probe. "Ah, not good." He pointed to the screen. See behind the receptor? It's a directional broadcaster; by the look of it, one that is in intermittent contact with several receivers."

"So what does that do?" Aran asked.

"I can't tell you the particular model from here, but normally they would be fitted to direct a signal to multiple receivers. Each receiver would expect to get a signal every so often; it might be every ten seconds, ten minutes, or even ten days. But if the receiver doesn't get the message, it normally switches off, or reverts to a default setting. I've known them used so that when a certain door is opened, the water-heater switches on, so by the time you arrive at the water-heater your beverage of choice is ready."

Taf looked at Aran. "Does that sound like a service provided by our eternally generous employers?" Aran's snort was answer enough.

Lian said, "Or if I was being paranoid, I would suggest that the receiver could be the detonator attached to an explosive charge."

The two SRCC techs stood thinking, and then Aran said, "Paranoid sounds sensible."

Taf asked, "So what do we do now?"

"I suggest you two suit up and cross to the shuttle. I will try and remove the board, but provide a substitute light source so the directional broadcaster doesn't realise. If this works, I can get the probe to attach a monitor to the broadcaster, find out directions, frequencies etc., and I can then try and locate the receivers and find out what they're attached to, and if possible, neutralise them."

"And if it goes wrong?"

Lian grinned. "You might just have to get yourselves a new satellite."

*****

An hour later, Lian, bulky in his armoured vac suit, was making careful adjustments to a cluster of light emitters on a stand. They formed a halo through which the computer board would be withdrawn, and were focused on where he calculated the receptor, which was invisible as of yet. The probe, still in place, he unhooked from the screen and plugged it into a small comms unit.

"Shuttle, can you read me?"

"We read you, Lian."

"Right, I'm about set up here. Can you pick up the probe?"

"Affirmative Lian, we've got it on the screen in the bridge and our two new passengers are sitting here with us, watching it."

"Right, I've voided this section to vacuum. I'm about to start the withdrawal and then I'm out of here. I'll unhook the line as I leave and you reel me in. Don't hang about, we don't want to be near here if it does go off."

"I hear you, Lian. I've got a man in our airlock to collect you."

Lian checked everything for the last time. He turned the key to wind up the little clockwork motor that would withdraw the computer board. He was glad the other two weren't present; techs always got unbearably patronising about the clockwork. But the little brass motor didn't produce sparks and he knew of no electronic countermeasures that could attack it. Finally he switched on the light array. Then he backed carefully out, watching as the board started to move, a mil at a time. Satisfied the process was working as he intended, he turned, stepped into the airlock, unsnapped the line from the holding bracket, clipped it to his suit, and jumped.

Ahead of him he could see someone in the shuttle airlock wave, and then reach up to start the line motor. He also saw the shuttle drives fire briefly. With his getaway secure he turned to watch the satellite receding beneath him. It hung there, much as he remembered when he arrived, the dull green enamel hull coat contrasting with the bright bronze of the airlock. Now his shadow, vague and somehow amorphous, moved slowly across the dust scared surface. He looked at the chronometer on his head-up display. The board should be out by now.

"Shuttle, can you read me?"

"Yes, Lian."

"What can you see from the probe?"

There was a brief silence then the voice spoke again. "It shows that the computer board has been withdrawn, and the area is flooded with infra-red." There was silence again, then "It looks as if you're hitting the receptor with infra-red."

"Now it all depends on how sneaky they were," Lian mused over the comm. He added. "If you're willing to spend the money, too much can be as bad as too little."

"Looking good at this end, anyway."

Lian grasped the handrail and pulled himself into the airlock. The outer door started to close, and Lian braced himself as the suddenly increasing acceleration pushed him to one side. With the pressure equalised Lian didn't bother to remove the suit, but travelled as swiftly as he was able to the bridge. The door was already opened for him, and he turned slightly sideways to fit through it. In front of him was the main screen. It glowed red and showed that the receptor was still being bathed in light.

"What's the view of the satellite like?"

Someone did something because instantly the screen showed the satellite hanging in space. "So far so good." Lian glanced across, it was Taf who'd spoken. Lian was just about to say 'give it time' when the satellite shuddered, and suddenly exploded. They watched in silence as chunks of satellite spread out through space behind them.

Lian said quietly, "Someone really didn't want you to know who tampered with the processor."

Aran was looking shocked. "And that would have happened if we'd just pulled the board out for routine checking?"

Lian tore his gaze from the screen. "It would have happened even if you'd just had a power failure."

Chapter 2

Haldar watched as Inspector Galway was led through the dining room towards him. He estimated that the inspector was in his late forties, early fifties, and his short hair showing the first signs of grey at the temples. He was of medium height, not perhaps as slender as he had been, and had a broad, plain but pleasant face. Then Haldar noticed the man's hands; they were long and narrow, with dextrous fingers. To Haldar, these were the hands of a craftsman or a weapons-tech.

Haldar had picked a table between two of the fountains: it was always pleasantly cool in summer, but more importantly, the sound of running water tended to baffle most commercially available eavesdropping devices. He stood up and shook hands as the off-worlder was introduced to him and gestured for him to take a seat.

"A pleasure to meet you Inspector Galway, how can we assist you?"

The inspector seated himself and looked round. "Well, first, call me Bartan. I get nervous when anyone calls me Inspector Galway; I half expect it to be the start of a formal reprimand."

"Bartan it is, but still, what can we do for you?"

"The New Charity Gendarmerie has a problem, and I'm afraid Tsarina is part of it. I was hoping we could assist each other."

"We always do what we can." Haldar stopped and turned to the young waiter who was hovering expectantly. "We'll have the set menu for two please, and could you bring a drink appropriate to the meal." He glanced at Bartan, "you don't have any dietary issues?"

"Well, nothing too heavily spiced, and if I have more than a couple of glasses of wine with my lunch I tend to doze through the afternoon."

The waiter made a note on his pad and left. Haldar felt that some explanation might be called for. "This place is staffed by students of the local catering college. The food tends to be good, the service brisk, and it is remarkably inexpensive."

Bartan gazed round. "It is rather impressive."

Haldar smiled. The dining room walls and ceiling were tiled in a rich blue, those on the ceiling showing streaks of green where they surrounded the circular domed roof lights. The tables were a white polished marble, the seats were chromed and the floor tiles were a white stone with gold and red veins running through it. There were four large fountains and around them were clusters of greenery. "It is amazing what you can do with good taste and a little imagination. Although," he added, "obscene amounts of money probably helped. It was built a century back and effectively bankrupted the Governor of the time. We're still paying off the loans."

The waiter returned with a tray and placed two plates and a carafe of wine on the table. "Your starter: A selection of breads, with small jugs of fish sauce, nut oils and balsamic vinegar. Good appetite, gentlemen."

Haldar thanked him, took a piece of bread and poured a little fish sauce on it. "The sauce is an acquired taste, but the nut oils and balsamic vinegar are excellent."

Bartan tried a little of the sauce on his bread. "I see what you mean, a shade hot for me." He poured some wine into his glass and sipped. "The wine on the other hand is really rather good."

Haldar poured himself a glass. "So, what is the problem?"

Bartan put down his glass. "New Charity is an agricultural world. A placid enough place; our rural officers tend to carry surveying tools to help them settle land disputes, rather than weapons. We have a fairly large, prosperous and conservative landowning class who prefer to spend their wealth on things which appreciate in value. Hence, we're probably one of the better markets for the excellent furniture produced in your town of Kenehan."

"I think at this point I'm supposed to congratulate you on the general sagacity of the population," Haldar said, "I only wish I could afford the stuff myself."

Bartan smiled a wry smile. "If I to start collecting it, I'm sure our anti-corruption branch would cast sharp eyes in my direction." He sipped more wine and tried some more bread. "We understand on New Charity that all Kenehan furniture is sold through the Kenehan Marketing Authority."

Haldar, his mouth full, just nodded his agreement. Bartan continued. "So when another company, Kenehan Independent Traders, started operating, we kept our eyes open. Obviously we got complaints from KMA, but KIT didn't seem to be doing anything illegal on New Charity, and we didn't get an official complaint from Tsarina. Anyway, this situation continued for five years: KIT sold quality pieces that slightly undercut the KMA pieces. But then we had a drugs bust. Do you have a problem with 'Abate' here?"

"Not that I know of," Haldar said thoughtfully, "should I be worried?"

"Probably not; Abate is a slightly addictive drug that produces very mild euphoria and contentment."

"I'm tempted to ask where I can buy it."

"Indeed, and if I told you that those taking it tend to be harder workers because they enjoy their work, what would you say?"

"Can I have enough for the entire department?"

"So say you and every other major employer. On the negative side, it reduces life expectancy, subdues libido, and reduces the willingness to face up to change." Bartan's tone was bitter. "So it is popular with employers and local politicians alike."

Haldar pushed his empty plate to one side, but kept his eyes on Bartan. "I get the impression it is not popular with you."

"Right," Bartan's reply was emphatic. "There are planets deeper toward the galactic core where whole populations are medicated with it. On the other hand, there are planets where anyone caught administering it faces the judicial punishment of being roasted to death on an iron griddle. Be that as it may, one of our rural officers became suspicious. He had seen the effect of the drug off-world. This was on a planet he left in a hurry when he realised that the authorities were conniving with the employers. Fortunately for us, when he saw the effects on New Charity, he had the wit to arrest someone and haul them to the labs so we could do a blood test. Because we knew what we were looking for, we found it. We raided the estate, found Abate, and proceeded to work our way back along the supply chain. It arrived on New Charity in furniture sold by the KIT. We raided them just as they unpacked a new shipment of furniture, and every drawer, every cupboard, was packed solid with sachets of the drug."

"Can you not scan for it?" Haldar asked. "I'd have thought that there would be a standard assay test kit for customs officials."

"Oh there is. But the various varnishes used in Kenehan are enough to bluff the scanners if you're casual and not really looking for the stuff."

"So did this Abate come from Tsarina?"

"We questioned people pretty intently, and threatened them with extradition to a less gentle judiciary. One of them claimed to have been to Tsarina. KIT had a presence on Akin. He met people in Purity, which he described as the financial capital, but he also said he'd been to the north, to what he called the Border Kingdoms. This is where he was shown the product and the production systems. So I thought you people might be interested." Bartan stopped and looked at Haldar intently. "Also, my superiors felt that my presence might encourage Tsarina to get to the bottom of this and clean it out."

Haldar sat silently. A young waiter cleared away the plates, and another waiter brought the next course, stewed sausages in a rich wine sauce poured over pasta. Haldar tried to fit Abate into a scenario involving porters and gun-toting bodyguards. He found this surprisingly easy; but women in surgical gowns? No, there were still gaps.

"Bartan, KIT never had an official existence here on Tsarina. KMA would have had them closed down. Still, we have issues in the Border Kingdoms. Perhaps your information answers some of our questions. I am about to travel there and would be pleased if you'd come along. Would that fit into your plans?"

Bartan nodded. "Yes. Not casting aspersions, but if I'm present during the investigation, my superiors are going to be a lot more willing to accept the findings; especially if they're *our* findings."

Haldar smiled. "Welcome aboard. Eat your dinner, and I'll tell you a story."

*****

Haldar booked them a cabin each on the evening steamer to Purity, the main city on the continent of Akin. Bartan approved of the mode of travel, having long ago rejected unnecessary flying. "It'll take three weeks for my report to get back and a further three weeks for any orders to come through, so why burn ourselves out with excessive haste?"

The journey was relaxed, the crew encouraged passengers to treat it as a pleasure cruise. Haldar suspected this might be to encourage more generous tipping, but agreed with the sentiment. They tied up in Purity before noon and Haldar phoned ahead to arrange a meeting with the Akin Trade Commissioner.

On the wharf, Haldar flagged down a cycle rickshaw. The driver was a wiry man, wearing the three-tasselled mortarboard of a Lay Brother of the Church of the Numinous Atmosphere.

"The 'House of Ritual Self-Mortification' please."

The driver nodded and beckoned Haldar and Bartan to climb into the seat. Once he had seen them safely aboard he stood up on the pedals to get the loaded contrivance moving.

"The 'House of Ritual Self-Mortification'?" Bartan's voice had a note of concern.

It was the rickshaw driver who answered him. "We keep the old names, but not the old practices. The Church sold it a generation or two back; it's all grand offices now, where the only bloodletting is a cutting memo. Still, at least they kept the old name; one can only live in hope that some of the good old ways will one day come back." He pedalled thoughtfully for a while before adding, "mind you, not having people hurl themselves off the roof of one of the more imposing buildings in the town centre has been pretty good for the people in my trade: more return fares."

The streets were narrow here, and paved with stone flags. The buildings were all set back from the road, surrounded by informal gardens where silk cotton trees and strangler fig wove through ruined follies. Flocks of iridescent butterflies made their erratic way between the trees. Most buildings they passed seemed to be built using opaque glass bricks in a score of different colours, some subtle, some harsher and more strident. Areas of colourless bricks seemed to act as windows.

The rickshaw stopped outside an impressive edifice. Haldar paid the driver and led Bartan along a path which wound through the gardens to the door. The front door led through a glass-lined tunnel into an atrium, where a receptionist asked their business, and then summoned an assistant to take them to the appropriate room.

She stopped outside a door on the upper floor. "Mr Wansaw's office; He's expecting you, please go in."

They found Mr Wansaw arranging flowers in a vase. "Ah Haldar, what brings you across to civilised parts?"

Haldar moved across and carefully adjusted a piece of driftwood and two ferns. "I think it needs the green forward, to be honest." He stepped back and looked, apparently satisfied. "Nothing much, just the Border Kingdoms as usual; what are they buying and selling?"

Wansaw brushed imaginary dust off his lapels. "You're in luck; I've managed to convince the university here to continue funding the economic research project my daughter has been doing for us for the last seven years." He moved to the desk, and pressed several keys on the keypad. A screen lit up on the wall behind him. "It's probably easier if I show you on this." He adjusted the focus slightly. "Look at the graph. First I'll display the income we know is going into the Border Kingdoms. It's money from the sale of minerals, agricultural products and similar. It's rising a bit, but they have spent money on a reasonably good genetic modification lab, with the aim of improving livestock and crops. They've also improved their mining technology." A dark red line appeared on the graph. It was virtually horizontal. "Now, this is a more speculative figure: tourist income and the sales of trinkets and gewgaws." A second line in a lighter shade appeared above the first. "Then we've got money remitted home by Kingdom citizens living abroad. This is assumed to be increasing as more of them go off-world." A third line, this time in blue, appeared on the screen. "Rough calculation means that the total is estimated to be this," which led to a fourth line, in black, appearing.

"A modest prosperity," Haldar observed.

"And this line is the amount they are spending. It's not hard data, but she collects what figures she can from customs records, with a generous allowance for smuggling. Then she adds a bit for the money their young bucks spend when they come here for the nightlife." A very broad fifth line appeared; yellow this time, considerably above the black line. "It's drawn so broad to allow for the fact that it is part data, part good estimate and part inspired guesswork."

Bartan asked, "Any idea where the extra money is coming from?"

"We did consider loans," Wansaw grimaced. "I don't think I've ever been subjected to as much scorn as when I started going round bankers asking if they'd lent money into the Border Kingdoms. We discounted savings and buried treasure. To be fair, in that area, they're probably synonymous and equally unlikely."

"Is the area peaceful?"

Wansaw shrugged. "Well, there are the usual assassinations, brigandage, even some raiding out of the Border Kingdoms into the rest of Akin, but really it is comparatively quiet. Also, I've included a standard figure for brigandage in the tourism total."

"And your conclusions?"

"They are getting money from somewhere, and frankly I don't think it is legal." Wansaw thought briefly. "Let me rephrase that, they're getting money from somewhere, and it isn't from their usual legal and illegal activities."

*****

Haldar flagged down another bicycle rickshaw. As they climbed aboard, Haldar asked Bartan, "What do you know about Akin?"

"Nothing really, only that the region is supposed to be a theocracy.'

Haldar muttered something to the driver, who started peddling. Sitting back in the seat, Haldar turned back to Bartan and picked up the thread of the conversation. "Yes. In the period before the fourth Governor was installed, the Church of the Numinous Atmosphere arrived. It was a bit messy; they were, as they put it, 'fleeing persecution.'"

Bartan looked intrigued. "So where did they come from and what did they believe in that led their neighbours to turn on them?"

"Well, initially they were militant vegetarians from Yargon III, a world somewhere further in towards the galactic centre. From what I remember being taught at school, they were very strong on not 'polluting the body' and this had all sorts of spiritual and ethical implications. Anyone who wasn't 'a believer' was a source contamination and had to be driven out, often with fire. Unfortunately, because of this dogma about not mixing with unbelievers, over time they became inbred and started showing some regrettable genetic diseases. Somehow, and I'm not sure if I was ever told how, they realised they had to broaden their population."

"Tricky if you're an inbred vegetarian cult," Bartan observed.

"Yes, they announced that vegetarianism was for the elect or inner core, rather than compulsory for anyone else. I suppose this would have worked, except that the elect insisted on remaining pure and uncontaminated. This was in spite of the irritating little detail that they had such severe problems; many of them were in need of regular blood transfusions. Because of this, new members were encouraged to give blood; a sensible idea, but somehow it got blown out of all proportion, and they were pilloried as some sort of vampires. Things escalated; perhaps their neighbours were jealous of the wealth of the church. Our history books tell us that the members of the Church took up arms to protect themselves and their investments. It seems to have gone badly. Finally, members of the cult escaped in three overloaded colony ships. These contained a few vegetarian Church members, and a very large number of cheerfully meat-eating lay members. The ships landed on Akin, and they managed to establish themselves. The locals objected, but by the time the Governor arrived and threatened to restore order, the Church was well dug in."

The busily pedalling driver looked over his shoulder. "The collected sermons of the Patriarch of the day are proscribed as outdated and heretical, and are therefore read by everyone. She preached widely on the text 'What we have, we hold'. She was a most convincing preacher."

"Not wishing to quibble, but shouldn't she have been a matriarch?" Bartan asked.

"She was proclaimed officially male by a convocation of elders," the driver explained. "That solved all *sorts* of hierarchical problems."

"So what's happened to these blood-drinking vampires since?"

With a glance at the driver, Haldar explained. "The sparse original population of Akin has either been pushed north into the Border Kingdoms, lurks as nomad herdsmen on the eastern steppe, dwells in small semi-independent coastal towns, or has just accepted the control of the Church."

"And the 'blood-drinking'?"

"Gene therapy, mainly, so that isn't really a problem anymore. The immediate problem for us is eating tonight. The prestigious restaurants are all vegetarian, because that is where the wealthy and well-connected eat. Or at least where those who wish to appear wealthy and well-connected eat. The food is excellent, pricy, and it is considered a mark of respect to the chef to break wind at some point during the third or subsequent courses. Or there are somewhat less prestigious places which serve a far wider range of dishes."

Bartan pondered briefly. "I'm not sure I could break wind with enough conviction. I suggest we go for somewhere with a less demanding code of behaviour."

"Good. We can get a hotel, a meal, and then we have to visit a nightclub."

"Are there no limits to the workload you pile on my shoulders?" Bartan observed. "A nightclub indeed; how respectable is it?"

Haldar smiled, "Disreputable enough to give our administrators palpitations whenever it appears on my expenses."

"Oh, I do hope so; New Charity is somewhat staid, and our administrators are easily shocked."

Haldar leaned forward and called out to their furiously peddling driver, "The Hotel of the Fourteen Lesser Virtues, please."

*****

Bartan felt that the hotel was entirely adequate. He confessed to himself that he was perhaps too phlegmatic with regard to his personal comfort, rarely making a fuss. But he still appreciated the better things in life when they came his way. This new world constantly intrigued him. On New Charity, he knew where he was with things. Food tended to be good, well cooked, perhaps a bit plain, but you knew what you were getting. The same with the people really, more crimes were committed out of pragmatism than passion. But here, everything was somehow more complicated. There were subtle currents that intrigued him, and he found the almost total lack of centralisation strange, but also stimulating. He thought of Haldar. He admitted to himself that he rather liked the Tsarinan. They were much of an age, and he had come to see that Haldar was a policeman to the core, even if the ex-service man hadn't admitted it to himself.

Bartan made his way down to dinner, and was amused to discover that one of the lesser virtues was 'Calculated Generosity'. A statue to the personification of the virtue had been placed where it could keep careful oversight of the plate the staff had put out for tips.

Their meal was excellent, thin slices of lemon-roast gastropod stacked between slices of blood pudding. It was interrupted when Haldar had to take a phone call. The phone had surprised Bartan; they were rare in the Wisp, where computer systems were seldom integrated, but Haldar had explained that, thanks to the SRCC, satellite phones were available on Tsarina, at least to a limited extent.

Haldar listened while Lian Gorfan was patched through to him from the shuttle. The marine described the events that had taken place at the satellite base station. Returning to his seat and putting his phone away, Haldar brought Bartan up to date with developments.

Bartan toyed with his glass. "So what we know is a transponder can come and go in your system and not be seen. Given that transponders can be cloned, there could be any number of ships coming and going."

"True enough, but we have to ask: why?"

"My guess would be they are smuggling something. Probably not Abate, or they wouldn't need to use Kenehan and the furniture route. But why destroy the base station?"

Haldar said slowly, "It doesn't destroy our communications; they use the individual satellites and don't pass through the base station. It doesn't impact on Military air traffic, either, and even commercial traffic can be handled by a jury-rigged control centre. We can get a ship in the correct orbit, and with the help of the SRCC, we'll have something running in a couple of days. So I would assume that it was because if we could see exactly how it had been done, we would know who did it."

"I suppose so," Bartan replied. "But back to the smuggling; what were they shifting?"

"I'm not sure, but I cannot imagine them shipping multiple shiploads of Abate. We'd be talking about tens of thousands of tons of the stuff; it wouldn't just be your people who noticed."

They sat in silence a while thinking, before Bartan said, "there were those women in the surgical gowns. Perhaps *they* were being transported."

"True, I'm having trouble fitting them into the picture. I don't think they were local women, I'm pretty sure I'd have heard something if they were. So it could have been the women who were being smuggled, but what on earth are they on Tsarina for?"

Bartan grinned, "I suppose we could always copy the archaeologists. If we don't understand something, claim it's part of a 'ritual activity'."

Haldar stood up. "Ok, we'll go for 'ritual activity' for now. However, we've got a night club to visit this evening."

Bartan stood up and glanced down at his semi-formal dress of grey side-buttoned jacket and matching flared trousers. "Am I appropriately dressed?"

"Don't worry; we're visiting, not performing."

With that, Haldar led the way down stairs and out through the foyer. They picked the bicycle rickshaw at the front of the rank, and as Bartan got in, Haldar said to the driver, "Padro's Place."

"That'll be extra, all uphill."

Haldar snorted, "Padro pays you boys a bonus for every punter you fetch him anyway, so don't give me that." He climbed up next to Bartan as the rickshaw jerked into motion. "Most clubs and hotels will give these boys a kickback for every guest they bring them; if you're young and fit you can earn serious money."

Bartan affected a small yawn and gestured towards their driver, "well, it makes me tired just to think about it, but it's kept him fit, there isn't an ounce of spare flesh on him." He turned to Haldar. "And what's this night club like?"

Haldar smiled. "You'll like it. I never met a policeman who didn't."

*****

The rickshaw deposited them at a tall building, nearly at the top of the hill overlooking the rest of Purity. The city fell away below them, glass buildings, dimly illuminated from within, skulked like gaudily-bejewelled ghosts among the trees. The trees themselves glowed with a cold light produced by carefully cultivated, symbiotic bioluminescent fungi. Bartan turned from the scene spread out before them to comment, "I wondered why I'd not seen any sign of street lighting."

Haldar said, "The people here have gone to a lot of effort to achieve the effect. The fungi spores are also bioluminescent, and they are released over one or two nights. When it happens, the whole city is delicately veiled in a thin cloud of light." He paid the driver and then he and Bartan walked in through the big double doors. A steady flow of people were passing in and out, under the eyes of four remarkably well-muscled doormen, resplendent in plush velvet pantaloons in coordinated pastel shades. Haldar led the way to a staircase and in a conversational tone said to Bartan, "we want the top floor: I need a word with Padro, who knows everything. Then again, there's someone else you ought to meet." He glanced across at a fifth doorman who stood at the foot of the stairs. "You remember me, Jango?"

Jango smiled broadly. "Oh yes, I remember you, sir. You got business with Padro?"

"If he'll meet with me, Jango, I certainly have, but is Kollette singing tonight?"

Again the smile; "she'll be on in five, ten minutes. I'll make sure Mr Padro knows you're coming."

"I'm sure you will, Jango. Anyway, we won't take any more of your time; it looks as if you're quite busy."

"Business is good, Officer Drom; all sorts of bad boys and girls with money to burn. You go up and see Padro."

The stairs were quiet; they seemed to be used mainly by staff. Haldar put it down to the fact that he was one of the few people who avoided the lifts in nightclubs.

At the top floor, they pushed through swing doors and the music hit them, loud, exuberant and with a heavy, driving beat that somehow promised excitement and action. They stopped and looked around. Half the floor of the main room seemed to be open for dancing; the rest of the room was filled with small tables, each with a couple of chairs. Off the main room, there were smaller rooms, most with doors fastened open. Haldar could see the card games and other entertainments. Bartan sighed happily, "I like this place already—it's just so sleazy and illegal."

Haldar nodded as he scanned the crowded dance floor. "That's Padro for you, sleazy, illegal, but strangely honest. He seems to want to give crime a good name." He gestured to the dance floor, "a good half of the men on that dance floor are from the Border Kingdoms, spending their ill-gotten gains. You can tell them by their weathered complexions, penchant for brown leather and some ritual scarring on the cheeks. A lot of the others are local ne'er-do-wells who hope some of the glamour rubs off."

"And the girls?" Bartan asked.

"Ah, the girls ...," here Haldar half bowed to a waitress in a flounced blouse and pencil skirt who came to lead them to a table. "The men in the Border Kingdoms regard marriage as a business partnership, which might produce children to carry on the business." He and Bartan sat down, and Haldar said to the waitress, "Two beers, from Padro's barrel." He turned back to Bartan. "Padro boasts of how he started out as a peasant boy making beer from grain he'd purloined from the drays. Even today, while the spirits are watered and the wine adulterated with gods alone knows what, he insists that the beer is good." Haldar ran his finger round the inside of his collar to loosen it slightly. "What was I talking about? Oh yes, the girls. A lot of them are drawn here because you have a lot of dangerous but exciting single men throwing money about. Their mothers may warn them against the place, but a fair number of girls who make a living hanging round nightclubs have been snapped up by a bright Border Kingdoms lad who spotted a sharp mind and iron will behind the short skirt and strappy top."

The lights dimmed, and the dance floor cleared. The waitress appeared with two glasses of beer and faded away into the gloom. Then one spotlight stabbed out, illuminating a woman standing alone in the middle of the dance floor. She wasn't tall, was probably carrying too much weight, but she somehow had a presence. Then in the darkness at the edge of the room came the first tentative notes from a xylophone. Now everyone was silent, listening as the first notes became chords and then other instruments joined in. Then the woman started singing. It was an old love song Haldar had heard many times before, but the power of the woman's voice, the sense of loss and longing, threatened to overwhelm him.

The voice fell silent, the last notes died away and the lights came up slowly. There was enthusiastic applause from around the tables, and the singer walked from table to table as if greeting old friends.

"Who's that?" Bartan's voice was hushed.

"Kollette."

"Ah. Now I know why the club is still open, and over-officious police officers haven't closed it down."

"Where else can you go to hear a voice like that?"

There was a cough behind them, and both men turned round to see Jango standing behind them, grinning. "I like working with Mistress Kollette," he said, "it's no trouble at all to sneak up on heart-broken middle-aged men."

Haldar threw up both hands. "OK Jango, you win, we're a pair of sad, old men with nothing to live for but the fluttering eyelashes of a nightclub singer."

"You and me both; still, Padro wants to meet you in his office. He said fetch your glasses, because he doesn't want someone else drinking your beer after you've been sobbing into it."

They followed Jango to a small open door at the edge of the bar. The door itself was blocked only by a heavy bead curtain. On the other side of the curtain there was a short corridor which turned sharp right and stopped at another door, this one activated by a key pad. Jango pressed keys and the door opened. Haldar looked at Bartan. "See the thickness of the metal?"

"Cut from a scrapped ship's hull," Jango said in passing, leading them down another corridor. He opened the door at the end and stood to one side.

"Your visitors, Mister Padro."

Padro was sitting on a couch, smoking a hookah. The style of the office itself was unexpected, the walls clad with rough stone for the first three feet, then plastered and whitewashed. Around the walls were hunting trophies; the place had the air of a Border Kingdoms hunting lodge.

"Gentlemen, so good of you to drop in," began Padro lightly, before continuing more guardedly, "what do you want, Haldar?"

"The wisdom of the ancients, or failing that, some of yours."

Padro shrugged. "You know me; you know what I don't talk about, so ask."

"The Border Kingdoms are spending money; they're into something that is almost certainly illegal. Any idea what?"

Padro put the pipe down and walked towards his desk. "I was rather expecting you. Have you seen one of these?" He picked up a heavy calibre rifle from behind the desk and worked the bolt. Then he ejected the magazine, glanced into the breech to check it was empty, and passed the weapon to Haldar.

Haldar examined it carefully. "Steel?"

"None of your ceramic and plastic nonsense. The stock is genuine wood."

Haldar worked the bolt and felt the weight of the gun. "Heavy, but very nicely made."

"I had some young buck from the Border Kingdoms owe me money. Anyway, he gave me that and offered me a few more to settle the debt."

"Have you fired it?"

"Oh yes." Padro sounded affronted. "I couldn't have one of these and not fire it. It is a beautiful hunting rifle, a joy to fire. The weight means that there is less recoil than you'd expect, though it is a heavy gun to carry on a long day."

"Ammunition?"

"It'll take commercial ammunition, but apparently they make their own, using cartridge cases made from copper coins."

Haldar passed the rifle to Bartan, who examined it carefully. "So much for black powder weapons only."

"The bolt action rifle is technology that was old before the birth of space travel," Haldar looked across at Padro. "Have they got automatics?"

"Well, they should be able to make them, but home-loaded ammunition makes them liable to jam, so I don't think they bother."

Bartan handed the rifle back to Haldar who handed it to Padro. "It's interesting; probably inevitable. But what else is going on up there? What else are these young bucks talking about?"

"You interested in anything in particular?"

"Well, you know me, Padro, I'm just generally curious. But seeing as how you asked, do you know anything about a drug called Abate?" Haldar thought he saw brief recognition in Padro's eyes, and then on an impulse added, "… and who is shipping the women and why?"

Padro raised the hand not holding the rifle. "Slow down a bit. Yes and no. Firstly, what is my standing at the moment?"

"The deal is still on, Padro. No one dies here, no one takes anything that does them serious damage, and the club stays open."

"Good, then we can do business." Padro sounded brisk; he laid the rifle on his desk. "There is more going on than I know about. But there is a drug being produced. It's being shipped out; it could well be Abate."

"Is anyone using it on Tsarina?" Bartan asked.

"Probably, but no one is talking about it. I got the impression they were really making it for export, but some bright lad might be using some on his labourers on one of the big estates."

"And the women?"

"That I know less about. But I know a little. A couple of years' back, one man from the Border Kingdoms got drunk and made me an offer for Kollette. That isn't unusual. But before his friends hustled him away, he said he just wanted to borrow her and make his own." Padro grimaced. "That is unusual, and I warned Jango."

"Why Jango?" Bartan asked, curious.

"She's *his* wife, and *my* sister. But we don't talk about it; it's good in this trade to be mysterious." A sudden smile split his face, then disappeared as Padro turned to Haldar. "Did you know?"

"To be honest, no; I wondered, but never tried to find out."

Padro turned back to Bartan. "She's not done badly for a farm girl from the other side of nowhere special, has she?"

"Anything else about the women, Padro?" Haldar tried not to sound impatient.

"Nothing, but we have been seeing strange people in here." He raised a hand to forestall the inevitable comment, "I know, but these were really strange. We are on the tourist trail; we're 'the expensive, sleazy nightclub where you can get a good time and be quite safe'. So I've had a lot of serious criminal types from all over the Wisp, some have even made me offers. But these strange ones were different. We had a group of acolytes from Castor VI. Now as far as I can tell, they are supposed to be sworn to chastity and don't drink. So what were they doing here, and why were they going into the Border Kingdoms? We had a party from Croton. They're way beyond the Wisp and from what I can work out they have 'A Glorious Leader' and take their cult of personality very seriously. There have been others as well. But what struck me was that visiting us seemed part of a sales package. Yet, only the sales reps seemed to be enjoying it."

Haldar took a map out of his pocket and spread it on the desk. "Given that they were on a tour, have you any idea where they were going?"

Padro shook his head and gestured vaguely at the map. "We just dropped them off at Jilwa Township."

Haldar peered closely his map. "Right, so Jilwa is here, a fly-speck town in the Border Kingdom of Bar-Khan." He turned to Bartan. "I think we ought to avail ourselves of one of Padro's other services."

"What would that be?"

"Padro, Bartan and I have some leave owing to us, and fancy a hunting trip."

"That can be arranged." It was now Padro's turn to be cautious.

"But we don't fancy tagging along with a group; we want one of your special trips."

"Just how special?" Padro had decided to be noncommittal.

"How close can you get us to here?" Haldar pointed to the map.

Padro looked carefully and indicated a spot not too far from Haldar's finger. "There is a small lodge there that we use. A hut, but it is quiet."

"When can you get us there?'

"The next scheduled flight to Jilwa Township is in two days, and from Jilwa it'll be a six day hike, but obviously you'll have porters."

"Padro ...," there was a hint of exasperation in Haldar's voice.

"Alternatively, if you want to breach the official restriction on private flights into the Border Kingdoms, I can get you to the hut tomorrow, late."

"A restriction on private flights?" Bartan interrupted.

Haldar nodded. "Yes, it's to stop the Border Kingdoms getting their hands on flitters, adding weapons to them and raiding even further south."

"A wise policy," Padro said, his tone sanctimonious.

"I'm glad you approve," Haldar said, dryly.

"I absolutely approve. It means that my legitimate competitors have extra costs... There have to be *some* advantages to being a criminal. Legitimate companies aren't expected to provide free holidays for law officers."

"We'll pay," Haldar said, hastily.

"Can you imagine what it'll do to my credibility if anyone ever discovers I've been taking money from your organisation? The last time I tried it, I had to wait three months for the vouchers; when I tried to cash them the department admitted it had no money anyway, and wondered if I could deduct the sum they owed me from my next tax bill." Padro looked scandalised. "Do I look like the sort of businessman who pays tax?"

"I suppose not," Haldar admitted. "Mind you, can you imagine the fight I have to go through to get your services on expenses?"

Bartan nodded sagely. "I think we just go, and Padro will doubtless come up with a favour he needs at some point in the future."

Padro allowed himself a smile. "I'll try; I'd hate to disappoint you both. I'll expect you here tomorrow, an hour before dawn. It's about the time I finish work. Oh, and don't worry, I'll provide hunting gear."

"Thanks," said Haldar.

Padro's smile got broader. "Thank me later, when you discover just what favour I ask for."

*****

When Haldar and Bartan arrived back, it was still dark, the streets were quiet, and bicycle rickshaws taking the last of the revellers home. Padro was waiting to pilot them in his own flitter. As they flew north and east, Bartan peered down into the darkness spreading out below them. They passed over the lights of the city, then the suburbs, until finally below them was largely dark.

Finally, sniffing appreciatively, Bartan said. "I'm finally beginning to feel at home."

"Why's that?" Padro asked, curiously.

"The subtle smell of night soil carried on the breeze," Bartan explained.

Padro waved a proprietorial arm, as if encompassing the entire plain. "I was born down there."

Haldar leaned over the side of the flitter and asked, "What are those lights?"

Below them were hundreds of tiny pinpricks of light, concentrated in a rectangular area, perhaps a thousand yards long and a hundred yards wide.

Bartan glanced down. "I'd guess they're little weeding droids. Are they Padro?"

"Yes, the lights are so you can find the damned things when you need to move them to the next plot."

"They're little things about the size of a fist," Bartan explained to Haldar. "Big enough to carry recognition software and pair of snips."

Haldar was still watching the lights in the darkness. "Why the parallel sides to the area they're working in?

Bartan asked Padro, "It looks like you use standard half-meter soil pipes."

"Indeed, then they feed into fifteen mil pipes running between plots and we use the usual commercial solar pumps to keep things moving."

Bartan nodded. "There's your answer Haldar, the pipes mark the sides of the plot. They serve a combination fertiliser and irrigation system. At least I'd assume irrigation, are there waste water reservoirs, so that you can dilute for irrigation purposes?"

There was pride in Padro's voice. "Yes, fertiliser and irrigation, but the reservoirs are buried, we don't waste land. The fifteen mil pipes take standard fittings so you just go in and set up the rain-guns when you want to irrigate a plot."

Bartan said, "I've moved rain-guns in my time. I assume that those down there have their own solar panel to power their pumps."

"They do." Padro smiled as he reminisced. "I used to move and service rain-guns before I made enough money to start my first night club."

"Jarado B14 Masticators in line to keep things chopped up fine and moving, stop the nozzles blocking?" Bartan asked.

"No, we use the big B145, but you only need one every twenty miles."

Bartan nodded to Haldar. "Ever seen a Jarado Masticator working?"

Haldar sounded a little bemused. "Unless they've taken to fitting them to warships, it's a branch of technology that's passed me by."

"They're impressive. They break things down so completely, they'll rupture cell membranes. They'll even break up waste wood that gets into the system."

"I suppose that's impressive."

"It is." Bartan glanced at Padro. "On New Charity, we reckon they'll break down a human body in a couple of minutes, and ten minutes later, the murder victim is spread over a hundred acres of wheat."

"Look," Padro said, "Haldar has a nasty, suspicious mind and doesn't need encouraging. How about we go down to ground level and take in the dawn?"

Bartan gave a broad smile. 'Now you're spoiling me. It might even keep Haldar from mentally running through his missing persons file to see how many have been recycled as fertiliser."

Padro brought the flitter down and landed it on a dirt road. He switched off the engines, and as they slowly stopped spinning, silence returned to the area. The three men sat quietly for some minutes, watching the first red glow appear on the underside of the clouds. The glow spread, reds, orange, even a hint of purple, and then there was the first rays of the sun. Day had broken.

Suddenly, there came the sound of a score of little motors starting up. Bartan tapped Haldar on the shoulder and pointed. On the nearest rain-gun, the solar panel was slowly rotating to face the east. Along both edges of the plot, a score or more of other rain-guns mimicked the action. As they watched, the sound of the motors grew louder, and then as Star MM43-62 showed her full face, all the rain-guns blasted a ruby laden coruscating fan of water into the air. The rain-guns of Akin saluted the dawn.

*****

In comparative silence, Padro flew them over perhaps a hundred miles of grain before he took them down, aiming at a somewhat grand house surrounded by gardens.

"Home?" Bartan asked.

"Yes, it's something I've managed to buy out of my savings." Padro glared at Haldar, "and it's a legitimate business. I declare my income and pay the tax that's owed."

"Tax owed on a farm?" Haldar sounded sceptical.

"I've got a good accountant, and it has to be admitted the last few years haven't been good ones ...," Padro broke off when Bartan started to laugh.

Padro smiled and brought the craft in to land in a less-grand courtyard surrounded by farm buildings that was set some distance from the house. They found a somewhat larger and more utilitarian flitter, its pilot chatting to a couple of mechanics. Padro introduced the pilot as George.

"And don't ask him what he used to do before he started working for me, or what his real name is."

Haldar and Bartan both looked suitably chastened.

George smiled shyly, "and if it's alright with you gentlemen, I won't salute either."

Bartan looked at Haldar. Haldar shrugged. "Probably best not to ask, let's just get our gear on board."

It took an hour or more before they were ready to depart. Padro insisted on watching them both fire the heavy Border Kingdom hunting rifles he had supplied. After emptying a magazine into a target at over three hundred yards, Haldar ran a cloth down the barrel to ensure it was clean. "They are nice rifles, Padro, a joy to shoot with." He held the barrel up towards the sun and peered through the breech to check that everything was spotless. Then he casually asked, "Selling many?"

"You never stop trying, do you? Believe it or not, they are a legitimate business, and the sales figures are with my accountant; obviously, the business will run at a loss, but that won't stop the tax authorities trying to demand their cut in due course."

Haldar closed the breech and held the rifle under one arm. "Don't be so touchy, they're a nice rifle. I'm intending to buy this one if you're selling."

Seeing the look of doubt on Padro's face, Haldar added, "Me buying it, not the office, so it'll be my money you'll avoid paying tax on."

"Get back in one piece first." Padro shook his head sadly. "I should have got you to sign a disclaimer, so I could prove to your office it was your own damned foolish idea.' Then he looked sharply at Haldar. "There is one thing. I assume you know, but perhaps not."

"Never assume I know," Haldar said. "What's the problem?"

"I never mentioned it, but there are rumours about the whole Abate business, rumours that it's political."

"Political?"

"Yes, some loudmouths from the Border Kingdoms have been putting the word out that they've got official backing, so not to cross them."

"Official? Are the Kingdoms running this?"

Padro spat on the flagstones of the courtyard; "Them, run anything? No, 'official' means it's at Tsarina Level; some of your own people could be involved in it, so be damned careful and watch your back."

Haldar was silent, his mind racing. Bartan asked, "I suppose there is no chance of names, or even hints?"

Padro shook his head. "Trust me on this. I actually like Haldar, he keeps his word. Also, I want paying for the rifle. But there are rumours that Tsarina Government people have been involved."

Haldar felt for his wallet. "Do you want paying for the rifle now?"

"No, just come back. There's something unpleasant going on, too many people who could make my life impossible are doing things up there. Sort it so an honest criminal can make a quiet living without having to worry about having his sister kidnapped."

*****

Haldar sat in the co-pilot's seat, Bartan in the crewman's seat behind. George quietly increased the thrust to the engines and the flitter moved gracelessly into the air and then gently accelerated. There was silence in the compartment and Haldar could sense tension in the air. He said, "Wallowing a bit?"

"She's well-loaded."

Haldar looked directly at the pilot. "So what is Padro playing at, *George*?"

Bartan picked up the emphasis on the name and asked "Am I missing something?"

"It's just that I don't know how many pilots Padro can get hold of, but he gives us one I've worked with before, and specifically tells me not to ask him questions," Haldar answered. "So, *George*, is it all right if I give Bartan here a short history lesson?"

"Be my guest."

Haldar half turned the seat so he could see Bartan and the pilot at the same time. "How about this, then; once upon a time, there was a dashing young naval officer called Doran Stilan; he was very popular, a gregarious sort of chap. Anyway, he met and married the pretty younger daughter of a wealthy manufacturer."

"A shrewd move," said Bartan, "Did he have debts?"

"Almost certainly, but as far as anyone could discover, it was a love match. Certainly they seem to be devoted to each other thirty years later, and no one has ever even hinted that one or the other has, shall we say, strayed."

"Most creditable," Bartan commented dryly. "And they all lived happily ever after?"

"It gets better. A year later, the older sister of Stilan's wife became the wife of Yakan, the widowed governor, and thus stepmother to the current governor Vladimir."

"So Doran Stilan became the brother-in-law of the Governor, and the uncle of the heir." Bartan's tone was expressionless.

"The much-loved uncle, by all accounts; and in spite of what you might think, Doran was considered a good influence on his teenage nephew."

"Can this sort of thing have an impact on a man's career?" Bartan's tone indicated that the question was purely rhetorical.

"Well, Doran's career didn't suffer." Haldar turned to the pilot, "George, which is the best warship in the Wisp?"

"The Taurus." There was no hesitation in the pilot's voice.

Haldar said "The Taurus, the pride of the Tsarina Navy, a system defence boat left over from the Salid Empire." Bartan could hear the pride in Haldar's voice. Haldar continued, "She was built with a heavy cruiser hull, but with no faster-than-light drive, which meant she could carry the armament of a small battleship. When the Empire was falling, no one could get a tug here big enough to take her away, so we've still got her." Haldar's voice was soft, almost reverent. "Everyone in the navy serves on the Taurus at some point, and to command her is the peak of an officer's career."

"You served on her?" Bartan had a feeling he already knew the answer to his question.

"Yes, I joined her as ensign, but made first lieutenant while serving on her. But then I was moved to Intelligence."

"So Doran commanded the Taurus?" Bartan felt he was going to have to keep digging, or Haldar was likely to drift off into reverie.

"Yes, he got his turn, perhaps ten years early, but it was a stepping stone to a job in the Diplomatic Service." Haldar looked at the pilot, who had remained grimly silent. "And how did he do as Captain, George?"

"He blew it."

"Perhaps you'd like to say a little more?"

The pilot spoke quietly, not taking his eyes off his instruments. His voice was conversational, but with a hint of bitterness. "To be fair to him, it may not have been entirely his fault. Every captain of the Taurus will get pestered to take such and such an officer. But being captain of the Taurus, they have the clout to ignore such requests. Perhaps being to an extent political, Doran was forced to return favours, or he might even have been pressured from above. But whatever happened, we didn't get the calibre of officers we should have—some of them were pretty bluidy average to be honest. On a normal tour it wouldn't have mattered, they were good enough to fly the boat. But then we had the incident of the Cornucopia." The pilot gestured to Haldar, "you tell him this bit."

"Bartan, does the name Wayland Strang ring any bells?"

"The Starmancer?"

"Starmancer, pirate, they're the same thing; but yes, he's the one," Haldar confirmed. "Although to be fair, you'd struggle to prove it in a court of law. Anyway, he was in command of a ship, 'The Predator.' He attacked the Cornucopia in the Tsarina system. A clear act of piracy, except, I think it was an insurance fraud."

"What makes you think that?"

"Well, the Cornucopia jumped into system at a point where its position was masked by the outer gas giant. Then the distress signal was broadcast on frequencies that were almost masked by a storm on the gas giant. Not only that, but the most valuable cargo was transferred remarkably quickly. It turns out to have been loaded last, and was right by the cargo hatch, already on pallets for ease of unloading."

"I see your point," Bartan said dryly.

"Well, it shouldn't have been spotted, but spotted it was, purely because the Taurus was loitering in the same gas giant. She got the jump on the Predator. That should have been it, but to give Wayland Strang his due, he thinks fast in a crisis. He managed to put the Cornucopia between him and the Taurus, then fired a spread of mines before running."

"Shouldn't be too tricky for the Taurus, the systems could surely track them and take them out."

"Now, that's what I would have thought. But what do you say, George?"

The pilot kept his eyes on the instruments, but the bitterness in his voice was more explicit. "The systems were off-line. Had been for days; we were waiting for spares. I'd spent the preceding three months jury-rigging them, they'd last a few more hours and blow, and I'd jury rig them again, and they'd blow again. I'd put in a request for the appropriate spares six months previously. I'd repeated the request three months later, and a fortnight before the incident, I'd made myself unpopular by telling the captain we wouldn't pass inspection, so *he* put in a request."

Haldar nodded and George continued, "Funnily enough, when the investigating officer checked, none of my requests could be found in the system; all that could be found was the captain's request." Then George paused briefly, "But here I'm getting ahead of myself. The Taurus was virtually blind; it had to fall back into the gas giant while the scanner crews frantically tried to get their systems back online. By the time they were, the Predator had gone. The Taurus was a laughing stock, and someone had to be blamed."

Haldar said to Bartan, "In navy slang, from time beyond memory, 'George' has been the name given to the officer you blame for things. A court of inquiry was convened and an investigating officer was chosen. The investigating officer did his best, and submitted his report to the court. It thanked him, marked his report secret, and blamed everything on George. Within weeks, the investigating officer was out of Naval Intelligence; fortunately he found a berth in the Governor's Investigation Office, because old Yakan knew when the wool was being pulled over his eyes. Within a month, Doran was promoted to the Diplomatic service, which he now heads, and there was a new Captain for the Taurus. I'm pleased to say that the new Captain took a whole fortnight to get the old boat back up to the sort of standard we expect of her." Haldar coughed, "but I'm running on again. We are left with George here, who faded quietly from the scene as if he'd never lived. Old Yakan wanted me to find George; the Governor hadn't liked the way he'd taken all the blame, but even I couldn't find him. Then suddenly, Padro hands him to me as my pilot." Then Haldar's tone changed, it became ostentatiously casual. "Bartan, have you noticed that our three chairs are on square floor blocks?"

Bartan was nonplussed, "I'm afraid I hadn't."

Haldar stood up and moved some of their kit that was stacked along the back of the cargo floor. "Yes, this looks like it. Pass me a bar, Bartan."

The pilot spoke. "No need for that. In the corner, there's a handle; it's in the bottom of the built-in tool box."

Haldar moved some more kit and found the toolbox bolted to the floor. He rooted around and finally found a handle at the bottom. He turned it ninety degrees, then gripped the floor edge, and the whole floor started to move.

The pilot adjusted the trim as he spoke, "it's not easy to open from inside, as you're standing on it. Best wait until we come to unload."

"So what's tucked away underneath?"

"According to Padro, a couple of tons of medium calibre caseless rifle ammunition."

Haldar looked genuinely surprised. "What's he planning, a small war?"

"I don't think he's planning one, it's just he has business partners who think one is about to break out."

Bartan interrupted, "Look, can you start from the beginning? I'm a stranger here. I was told the people up in the Border Kingdoms were using black powder, and now you're selling them modern ammunition for a war that no one has mentioned."

"Alright, how about this," said George. "The craftsmen in the North have always been making nice firearms, but ammunition is a problem. Making smokeless powder is tricky. Well, perhaps ten, fifteen years ago, they cracked it. Hardly surprising—they've got local kids who've gone on to become college graduates in Purity. But from a military point of view, they still have problems. Effectively, they cannot get the quality reliable enough for automatics, but they make good bolt-action hunting weapons." The pilot stopped as if he were thinking. "But that's a blind alley. The real change came about five years ago; someone came in with money, and started making Abate. OK, so we didn't know it was Abate back then, but that's what they were making. They got really friendly with Bar-Khan, which is one of the more northerly Kingdoms. They set up their kit in one of the more isolated valleys, and the money flowed in. Anyway, someone got ambitious and started working on other things. I've been listening to some of the people I've shipped north. Now there is a genetic lab up there, and they're not just working on livestock. So the money is still flowing in, faster now, and other people have to be paid off. Bar-Khan has quietly absorbed a couple of valleys along the border, and some of the other kingdoms have started to get nervous. Some have been bought off, some were threatened and others decided to find friends. Recently, one of Bar-Khan's neighbours, Gal-Khan, approached Padro. They want him to supply them, and they are willing to do favours."

Haldar broke into the flow of information, "what about Padro and his talk of government people involved?"

"I've been into Bar-Khan, I've seen Watch Company personnel there. I assume they still exist to provide the Diplomatic service with embassy guards and a small rapid reaction force."

Haldar's tone was contemptuous when he replied, "they do. But some of us regard them as Doran Stilan's private army. I think a doting nephew let him have a few soldiers to play with so his uncle could still wear a military uniform."

"Well," the pilot continued, "your friend and mine, Doran Stilan, is fishing in some interesting waters, and making an awful lot of money, and probably upsetting some interesting people."

Bartan butted in, "Who's he upsetting, apart from us?"

"Do you know who had control of what little Abate used to be available?"

"Afraid not," Bartan admitted.

The pilot grinned evilly. "Wayland Strang was a smuggler before he ever aspired to be a Starmancer. I don't know if he manufactured the stuff, but he took a big cut from distribution. Doran Stilan will be costing him serious money."

Haldar sat, thoughtful. "So why didn't Padro just tell me this, or has he promised people he'll hold his tongue?"

"He's trapped between Doran Stilan, who could close him down legally, and Wayland Strang, who could probably cripple him, but illegally. So he hopes that you will sort this. The fact that there could be a war, and that Abate is politically serious bad news, is the bait to get you involved. He'd doubtless apologise for not being up-front with you, but he *is* a criminal. There are things he cannot afford, and too much honesty is one of them."

Haldar looked across at Bartan. "What a bluidy mess."

Bartan shrugged. "If this job was easy, they'd probably not bother paying us at all. So what do we do?"

"I think we might as well go in and have a look. If needs must, it might not be too difficult to close the operation down, but it will have to be done properly. The big problem is Doran Stilan. He is out of my league; he's close to the Governor. While I don't think Vladimir is involved, he could be politically damaged, so some tact is called for." Haldar turned to the pilot. "Do you think Doran is trying to get his own back on Wayland Strang?"

"I don't know. Perhaps he is just thumbing his nose at him."

"What will Strang do?" Bartan asked. "He is a big operator, he could take the hit, but it would lose him credibility."

George answered, "I think he'll react, and if Doran Stilan is trying to get his own back, it might be that this is part of Stilan's plan. When Strang reacts, he gets a bloody nose. After that, if word gets round that Doran Stilan has out-thought him, a lot of Strang's captains might decide to cut ties with him."

Bartan sighed. "Looks like we have a pleasant walk in the mountains ahead of us, then."

*****

The hut was tucked away in a valley off a valley, almost hidden in plain sight, its stone roof and walls the same colour as the surrounding rock. George landed next to it and helped them unload their supplies and luggage. The hut was less commodious than the hunting lodges Haldar remembered seeing in the brochures, lacking staff, under-floor heating and running water, but there was a fireplace and their supplies included a quantity of coal. Bartan looked round the one room. "A little on the primitive side perhaps?"

George opened a box. "We have yak hide boots, yak hide parkas for two, yak hide leggings, and yak hide sleeping bags."

"I take it that yak hide is the new black?" Bartan held the parka against him. "It's a bit large..."

"You wear it over your normal clothes."

Haldar tried his on. "If I remember right, this is the standard local garb."

"Yes, everyone hunting in these mountains wears this sort of thing." George rooted around in the box. "Ah, just the thing. Yak tallow, for rubbing into the boots and the stitching in your parka; it'll keep them waterproof." He dropped the tin back into the box. He took one of the heavy, hooded jackets and held it up to examine it more closely. "Yes, he's got you Bar-Khan garments. You can spot them because they tend to use darker hides for the hood. Once in Bar-Khan, they'll mark you out as one of their own; this side of the mountains, you'll just be a viable target."

"Oh, good," said Bartan, "at least we'll know why people start shooting at us for no apparent reason."

George just laid the parka down on the table. "Up here there will always be someone shooting at you. At least wearing Bar-Khan clothing they'll get close enough to check who you are." He opened another box. "Self-heating ration cartons."

Haldar leaned over his shoulder to look. "Military surplus? I always liked the ones which included chicken, even if the '*chicken*' was really gastropod."

George shook his head. "Local manufacture; they use a carton rather than a can. You can use the cartons as kindling to light your fire." He looked at the labels. "No chicken, just a hundred different ways to cook elderly yak. You might find them a bit heavy on the sauce, and a bit light on the meat, but between us, once you've eaten the meat for as long as I have, you'll prefer it that way round."

Haldar took a carton and read the nutrition information: "May contain trace quantities of hallucinogenic lichen?"

"There was an unfortunate incident some years ago. Elderly yaks of the sort which tend to grace ration cartons will survive the winter by eating the lichen off a rock-face. Some of the lichens have strange properties, but yaks have a high level of tolerance." George cast a last eye over the scene. "Anyway, I'd better be on my way; I'd really like to get down out of the mountains before dark. It smells like there could be snow coming, too."

Haldar started laying the fire. "Makes sense. When do we see you next?"

"When you call me, but it could be a day or more before I can collect you; depends on where exactly I am." He buttoned up his jacket. "We tell our customers to book early to avoid disappointment." Pausing at the door on the way out, he added, as if it was an after-thought, "Oh, something might be happening in five or six days' time. I can normally tell because of who is moving. There might be a ship coming in."

George left, closing the heavy door behind him. A few minutes later Haldar and Bartan heard the flitter motor stutter slightly, then there was a growl as George applied enough power to take off and leave. Bartan selected two cartons and read the instructions. "Remove lid, pull tab, when carton turns red, eat."

As he obeyed the instructions, Haldar sorted through his luggage and by the time Bartan served the meal, Haldar had managed to cover the hut's only table with a map built up from satellite photographs. As they ate, Haldar pointed out a route.

"We want to climb a fair bit, get onto this ridge, and from there make our way into the deeper massif. Here, three valleys over, we start to hit the gorges, and here," Haldar prodded the map with his spoon, "is the gorge where the journalist's flitter was shot down."

Bartan studied the map. "I see the gorge opens out at its northern end."

"Yes, and there's a large village there. I think it would be interesting to visit the village and then go down into the gorge to look for bits of the flitter."

Bartan sounded surprised. "Hasn't someone been in to collect the bodies?"

"There was no emergency beacon; the only reason we know about the crash is because we were intercepting their signals. So hopefully the locals think they've got away with it."

Haldar traced another path with his spoon. "We can reach there by taking a longer route through the central massif."

Bartan tried to assess the distance. "Two days?"

"Perhaps three."

It took four, and there was light snow every day.

Chapter 3

Bartan shrugged off his pack and joined Haldar sitting under a rock overhang. The snow had turned to rain, which had slightly improved visibility. Haldar reached into the pack he was carrying and pulled out two cartons.

"Probably time to eat."

Bartan took the carton, removed the lid and pulled the tab before setting the carton down on a rock. "It has to be admitted, the paths are easy to find in the rain." He looked down at where a small stream hurried past them. "I suppose all the paths are streams."

Haldar looked up from his own carton. "Yes, but not all streams are paths. I think that's where we went wrong this morning. We climbed too soon and too steeply."

Bartan pulled his spoon out of his belt and started to eat. "Stewed yak and beans with chilli."

"They're all stewed yak and beans with chilli."

Bartan shook his head. "No, I'm sure some have different spices. I had one yesterday that was quite mild; this morning's was almost sweet."

"I'm not convinced. I think they make them all in the same vat, and just don't make too much of an effort to stir it."

They ate in silence; when they had finished, each crumpled up the carton and stowed it back in his pack for the evening's fire.

Bartan sat and looked back at the way they had come. The rain had lessened behind them and the sun was starting to break through. He had the feeling he could see forever. The col on which they rested fell away in front of him. He was looking down a long valley, its walls almost sheer. One side glistened where the weak sun managed to shine through a break in the cloud, the other wall indistinct, black rock lost in shadow. At one point he could see a stream flow over the edge of the cliff and plunge into the chasm below, the water briefly turned into a shower of droplets which were surrounded by rainbows of refracted light.

"I think the rain has slackened a bit, we might be in for a spell of nice weather;" Haldar said, not sounding entirely convinced. Loose stone crunched under his feet as he stood up.

Bartan shouldered his pack and picked up his rifle. "Whether it has or not, we might as well keep moving."

Haldar looked at his watch. "Four hours till dark. We've got to find somewhere to shelter for the night." He stood up and looked west. "That might be the path we want, to the left of that crag." A squall blew across and the crag was lost in the rain. Haldar struggled into his pack and slung his rifle. "Or perhaps not; who knows in this gods forsaken country?"

*****

On the fourth night, they slept in a boulder field, a sheet of camouflaged fabric stretched between two rocks in lieu of a tent. The rain and snow had at last stopped, and the night was clear, bright, and bitterly cold. Before they turned in, Haldar and Bartan made their way to the edge of the boulder field where the ground fell away, and looked down on the village far below. Haldar drew a slim vision enhancer from his pack and peered through it.

Bartan asked, "How do we get down without being seen?"

Haldar stood in silence for some time before answering the question. "I suggest we sleep now, watch tomorrow and walk down tomorrow night when it's dark. Just hope that we're the only people with night-vision goggles."

Bartan peered through his own vision enhancer. "What exactly are we looking for?"

"Hard to say; I've spent a lot of time trying to get satellite footage of this valley. I had to get footage from a Marine Orbital, but even with passive microwave scanners to get through the cloud, I couldn't see all that much." Haldar gestured with his left hand. "Looking at the ground, can you see the road which runs from the village down into the gorge? My guess is that whoever is bringing a ship in can take it down into the gorge where it would be easy to hide."

"I see the road. It goes into the centre of the village and then stops at what might be a village square."

"That's the one," Haldar agreed. "But this village is interesting; I managed to get some of the old maps, and it isn't marked at all. Not that that means a lot—maps of the Border Kingdoms are apt to show villages and even towns that come and go between editions."

"Isn't there any census data?"

"Census data?" Haldar appeared amused. "We don't even have census data for Kaunas City."

"So how does the government plan for anything?"

"I think you've got the wrong idea about the government here on Tsarina. Our early Governors went back to first principles. They decided that the main purpose of a bureaucracy in general is to provide jobs and salaries for the bureaucracy; bureaucrats spend just enough on the rest of the populace to justify their existence. Eventually, the bureaucracy will grow large enough to be self-sustaining. It can justify its existence purely by existing, and promotion opportunities can be created by generating a further structure which exists to monitor the bureaucracy. Eventually, you get to the situation where the bureaucracy swallows all the funding, and none is left for those functions the bureaucracy was created to administer. These functions end up being outsourced to voluntary agencies which are reduced to being an unpaid branch of the bureaucracy, with further tiers of bureaucrats hired to monitor their performance. They decided to manage without one, if they could."

"You don't like bureaucracy do you?"

"We manage without it. Actually, we couldn't afford it. A planetary government cannot technically go bankrupt, but we run it pretty close. The Governor supports the military and handles planetary defence. This he does out of a private income and an import duty, plus a fixed voluntary contribution from all the autonomous regions. Each region has the level of government it wants. By the time we've paid for the military, there is rarely any left, so the Governor's office lives from hand to mouth. But I get paid on time most months, and we manage after a fashion."

"But you don't know when this village appeared."

"That is because someone has selectively deleted some of our stock of satellite images."

Bartan was silent. Then he said, "Someone is at least thorough. Are there any others missing?"

Haldar laughed. "Plenty; some misfiled, some used for something else. I once discovered the complete set covering Kaunas City and surrounding area being used as a backdrop for a school drama performance."

"You people don't take this whole record keeping thing seriously, do you?"

"Of course not! Who in their right mind tells the state their business? It would only tell you to stop doing things."

Bartan shook his head in mock disbelief. "How about we eat and then get some sleep? Tomorrow could be a long day."

*****

The next day dragged. It wasn't just that nothing happened; it was that it didn't even look as if anything was ever going to happen.

"Noon, let's eat."

Bartan pulled himself up into a sitting position. "I'm not sure I can stand the excitement. Just how much spice will there be in today's *Yak and Beans Surprise?*"

"I had a look in one of the other boxes. There are cartons of mixed fruit dumplings." Haldar held up a coloured carton with pictures of fruit on it.

"Let's live a little. Break out the dumplings; spare no expense."

Haldar passed him one of the cartons. Bartan took the top off and pulled the tab. The filling of the carton seethed and roiled for some minutes, and then Bartan prodded the contents with his spoon. Cautiously, he tried a spoonful. "Well, the spice is different, and I don't think there are any beans."

Haldar eyed his carton suspiciously. "Apparently the dumplings are made from the finest yak suet."

"You know where you are with yak," Bartan observed, trying a second spoonful. "Not sure about the fruit, it seems to be generic fruit rather than a named species." He proceeded to eat in silence.

Haldar continued to stare at the village below them. "I think there are several things we can say about the village. Firstly, there are no women or children, or indeed anyone at all wandering about during the day."

"Agreed; so whatever it is, it isn't just an ordinary village."

"Secondly, the ground it is built on looks remarkably flat, and there is a level area to the south of it at the head of the gorge with a few fields of grain growing on it."

Bartan finished chewing another mouthful of dumpling. "This is the largest area of level ground we've seen for days. So it may have been artificially levelled."

"Thirdly, there are paths up both sides of the valley, which don't reach the top, and end in nondescript rock formations."

"Yes, and gods alone know what is going on there."

Haldar stirred his carton and tried another spoonful. After chewing for some time he swallowed and said, "One of those formations is probably a couple of hundred feet below us. Would it be worth checking it out on the way down?" He left the question hanging in the air.

Bartan sat and looked out over the valley. "I'd rather we find out what it is and then avoid it, than bypass it and leave whatever it is along our line of retreat."

Haldar leaned back against a rock and glanced up at the sky. "It's clouding over again, heavy cloud. I think we take turns to sleep off the dumplings and then move down when it gets dark."

*****

They waited for it to grow dark, getting used to the night-vision goggles before they started moving. The setting sun caught the underside of the cloud sheet, briefly painting it with a score of variations on red; then the sun was gone and everything was dark. The fall of night was accompanied by a light, steady snowfall. They followed a game trail that ran almost straight down the side of the valley to the suspect rock formation below them. Just above the formation, Haldar, who was in the lead, halted. Bartan stopped some paces behind, and Haldar turned and hissed to him, "Put your hand on the rock."

Bartan did and felt a slight vibration. "What's happening?"

"I think there is a big power source somewhere."

"Big?"

"Big!" Haldar's tone was decisive. "Bigger than the shield generator on the old Taurus, anyway."

"Haldar, you're talking to a simple farm boy here."

"OK, big enough to power a village larger than the one below."

Haldar moved slowly forward. He stopped and sniffed. "Can you smell yak?"

"This is where the farm boy comes in. I can smell something, and I'd say vaguely bovine." Bartan moved left of Haldar and listened. He whispered, "There is something to the right, just below us."

He went down on his hands and knees and crawled slowly forward, thankful of the sparse grass that protected him a little from the rocky ground. He halted and raised a hand, beckoning Haldar to join him. "Quietly."

Haldar knelt beside Bartan and looked where Bartan pointed. There was a path cut deep into the rock beneath them, separating them from the main outcrop. Below them, they could see light stream out of an open door, and someone was leading yaks out onto the path. In silence, the two men lay and watched. Finally, a dozen yaks were gathered below them, saddled, bridled and ready to ride. The light snow was settling on their long, matted coats. Haldar whispered in Bartan's ear. "George said that something might be happening."

They lay together in silence and waited. Below them, the yaks waited patiently. Occasionally, there was the shuffling of feet or the sound of one scratching its head on the rock wall of the path. After perhaps half an hour, both men could hear the deep drone of a sub-light drive. Bartan looked up and pointed. To the north, through the snow, a spaceship was coming in low, at just over stalling speed. Immediately, men spilled out of the door below them, joking and laughing, mounted the yaks and rode off down the path.

As Bartan and Haldar watched, the ship passed above the village and continued slowly down the gorge. Below them was silent. Bartan glanced at Haldar. "Do we take the path?"

"It could be the fastest and least conspicuous way down."

Gingerly, Haldar slipped over the edge and made his slow way down the deep slope to the path. Once he was at the bottom, Bartan followed. As

Bartan's feet touched the path, Haldar peered cautiously though the door of the stable. "No one here, but there is another door."

He slipped inside and cautiously approached the second door. Listening carefully, he eased it open.

"Problem?"

Haldar was addressed by a bored-looking man wearing what looked like Watch Company fatigues with the badges removed. Haldar glanced about. There were four men in there, all wearing similar fatigues, even down to the dark patches where badges had once been sewn on. The other three were doing the pre-firing checks on a pulse laser, and were largely ignoring him. In a gruff voice Haldar said, "Gloves?"

The bored man looked round the floor. "None here."

Haldar raised his hand in a gesture of thanks and backed out of the door, closing it behind him. He turned back to Bartan who slipped the safety catch back on his rifle. Haldar gestured that they get out and Bartan stepped back onto the path.

"What did you find?"

Haldar's tone was casual to the point of exaggeration. "Only a pulse laser, with four crew in Watch Company fatigues."

"A pulse laser? Aren't they fitted on spaceships?"

"Only on big ships; no wonder there is a big power source somewhere."

"So what now?"

Haldar considered briefly. "Down, I think. We really want some answers—all we've got is a selection of excellent questions."

*****

They made their way down the path, Haldar in front, both men now carrying their rifles ready for use. They had marched for around two hours when lights appeared, coming out of the gorge. They stopped and studied the area through their vision enhancers.

"A column of people?"

Bartan fiddled with the focusing. "Could be; hard to tell with this snow. If it wasn't for the lights, you'd not know they were there at all." He studied the scene again. "Women?"

"I'm guessing as well but I think you're right. There are also some riding on yaks."

"Our friends from up here?"

"It would make sense: guards used to escort whoever it is."

They continued on down the path, dropping steadily, and were now barely a hundred feet above the village. Haldar suddenly stopped again and pointed.

"Look at the main hut in the village; it looks as if someone has opened a door."

As they watched, a column passed out of the hut and trudged through the snow towards the gorge.

"Women; and they're wearing those surgical gowns we saw in the reporter's footage. Gods, they must be cold."

Bartan scrutinised the distant figures through his vision enhancer. "One lot comes in, one lot goes out. Obviously, today is some sort of change-over."

They waited and watched. The two columns passed each other. One disappeared into the gorge, and the other made its way into the village and disappeared into the main hut.

Haldar said quietly, "Let's get closer."

They moved onwards, but were soon down to the level ground. They worked their way along a shallow gully cut by a stream, which brought them to the edge of the village. At one point, they lay flat as a party a dozen strong rode along the track above them.

Bartan tapped Haldar on the shoulder. "The escort going back?"

"Could be."

They waited in silence for perhaps twenty minutes, until Bartan said, "I can hear something; is that the ship leaving?"

"Could be. I'd expect it to."

Something was illuminating the gorge from within. Minutes later, the ship moved slowly out of the mouth of the gorge and then accelerated upwards, disappearing through curtains of snow blowing across the valley.

Haldar crawled up to the level of the track. "How about we just walk down the track? We'll have to do something soon, and the snow will shield us from casual observation."

"Won't we be a bit conspicuous?"

Haldar looked at his companion. "We've not washed, shaved or put on clean clothing for the best part of a week. We're too old to be the lead singers of a young persons' light music combo; I suspect we'll probably pass for local huntsmen."

"Makes sense." Bartan clambered up, and the two men, their rifles slung casually over their shoulders, walked nonchalantly down the track towards the village. As they passed the first house, Haldar stepped into the shadows and peered into a lighted window. He beckoned Bartan across. "Look, through the window. There is just a light behind the glass; the actual building appears to be solid."

"An interesting architectural style. Popular in the Border Kingdoms?"

"Won awards for it, they have. Second-hand roof slate so the building looks old from above, new stone for the walls that no one can see from above and a solid concrete interior. Wears well and cheap to rent."

They carefully made their way around the house.

"A door."

Bartan peered past Haldar. "Opening it?"

Haldar gingerly grasped the handle and pressed down with his thumb on the old-fashioned latch. He pulled and the door opened easily enough. Inside, all was dark. Haldar allowed his night-vision goggles to adjust, and could make out the lines of another door set into a concrete wall. He pressed the control panel and the door soundlessly fell back out of sight. Light flooded out of the space behind.

"Quick, get in and shut the outer door behind you."

The two men scrambled through the second door, Bartan closing the outer one. They both took off their goggles and allowed their eyes to adjust. They were at the top of a spiral staircase. The steel stairway wound down out of sight.

Bartan made a gesture of elaborate courtesy. "After you my good man."

Haldar bowed back. "If you insist."

Rifle at the ready, he made his watchful way down the stairs, Bartan following him perhaps six steps behind.

They came to a landing off which ran a long corridor, clinically lit by concealed lighting. The stairs continued to wind downwards. Haldar glanced over his shoulder. "I suggest we check out the corridor first."

Bartan nodded his agreement. "Look like we're supposed to be here, and see if anyone appears to stop us."

The two men crossed the landing and peered down the corridor. It was empty. Although aware that their current guise could seem incongruous in these ostentatiously clean surroundings, the two men walked, apparently casually, down the corridor. Bartan stopped and pointed to a plate set into the wall. "Grorin-Tech modular medical construction."

"Grorin-Tech?" Haldar looked from the plate to Bartan. "Don't think I've ever heard of them."

"They might not get this far out. New Charity has had dealings with them. They do a lot of medical tech, modular labs, and wards, whatever. Slot it together and switch on the power and you're up and running."

"No, I've never heard of them." Haldar was definite.

"Strange bunch, more a tribe or clan than a company; they are reputed to be based on a wandering planet drifting deep in the empty space between solar systems."

Ahead of them, a door whined open. Haldar raised his rifle as someone entered the corridor, but Bartan placed his hand on the barrel to gently push it down.

"Look carefully."

Haldar watched as a man stepped into the corridor. At first he thought the man was wearing some sort of complex exoskeleton. The Taurus had a couple of them for cargo loading, and like other young officers, he'd trained on them. But then he realised the man was not wearing the exoskeleton, but was an integral part of it. There seemed to be little more than a head; the neck and torso were concealed within some sort of sac suspended in the exoskeleton. The man glanced incuriously at Haldar and Bartan, turned and walked deliberately down the corridor away from them. Haldar turned back to Bartan. "So what was that?"

"Grorin-Tech also supplies lab-techs and even medical staff if you are willing to pay for them." Bartan wore a look of distaste. "Apparently, it was decided by our authorities not to take them up on that particular offer."

"So what are they then?"

"From what I've been told some are serious accident victims that have been given a 'second chance'; others are condemned men paying off their debt to society."

"Condemned? What for?"

"For being inconvenient, perhaps? They offered to take our convicted criminals, pointing out that it was an economical way for us to dispose of them." The dislike in Bartan's voice was palpable. "There are modifications undertaken within the brain which will remove much of the personality and cancel out other traits. The sales brochures were quite glowing about the quality of the results."

Bartan stepped forward and looked through the open door. He beckoned to Haldar to join him. "Here, they obviously bought the full package. Haldar, three more working in this lab. I wonder if they have the full medical team as well."

Haldar looked round the lab. Three more individuals, more or less modified, were engrossed in various complex tasks. One consisted of a gantry, among which an arm moved, titrating precise quantities of reagents into the tubes arrayed below it, the movements apparently coordinated by a head, set into some kind of white ceramic vessel which was mounted on a separate gantry rail. "This isn't telling us a lot. What would they do if we just went in and looked at things?"

Bartan shrugged, "if we moved something they were working on, they might react; otherwise, probably not an issue."

"Let's move on, see what else there is here; distasteful and immoral are not necessarily illegal," Haldar suddenly grinned, "otherwise I've got my 'ex' bang to rights."

The two men continued down the corridor. There were more doors, some of them opened as various lab-techs moved in and out, oblivious of all save their errand. Bartan said quietly, "Ever busted a drug lab?"

Haldar shook his head. "There's only small neighbourhood stuff, the local authorities deal with that."

"I've done a couple. I'd say we have a manufacturing lab." Bartan stopped as the next door opened. A trolley came through, being manoeuvred by a lab-tech with no visible face. On the trolley were rigid cartons. Bartan picked up the top carton, opened it and showed it to Haldar.

"Packed into sachets, each looks to be a set dose for a given number of people." He peered at the side of the carton. "Yes, here it says 'Abate, two hundred and fifty sachets.'"

Bartan pulled out a sachet, "even got the dose on, 'One sachet for ten adults per day.'" He put the sachet back in the carton and placed the carton back on the trolley. The lab-tech adjusted the carton slightly and continued on its way.

Bartan looked round. "I'd say this is a standard layout, so there will be lifts in the middle of the corridor, and another spiral stairway at the far end. No cameras, so I assume they haven't bought the security package. I wonder if they have the maintenance package."

"What does the maintenance package involve, or do I not want to know?"

"You probably don't want to know. If they've bought the full package, there will be a clan of three-foot-tall humanoids somewhere. Our authorities classified them as non-human domesticated animals; they have an aptitude for the equipment and they appear to train their young to continue to service the facility."

Haldar shook his head. "Let's just find out what else is going on and get out. This place is beginning to sicken me." He changed his grip on the rifle and added "we still haven't found where the women are being taken to."

"We'll go along the corridor and down the stairs that are probably at the far end." He led the way, occasionally peering through open doors as they passed. "Looks like all labs on this floor."

When they reached the second stairway, Haldar halted.

"Why haven't we met any guards or other security?"

Bartan turned to him, "They didn't buy the security package; that much is obvious. Perhaps they felt location and guards on the outer perimeter were adequate. Perhaps the guards were pulled out to deal with the transfer. Or maybe they're keeping out of the snow somewhere cosy."

Haldar grunted. "Perhaps they're downstairs, looking after the important stuff."

Bartan gave a resigned sigh. "We might as well go and find out. After you."

Haldar made his way down the stairs as silently as possible. The lighting was dimmer here, dim enough for him to pull the night-vision goggles back over his eyes. At the landing, he halted. The stairs continued downwards into total darkness. Haldar glanced back at Bartan. "You're used to this sort of set-up. Down or try this level?

"If it's totally dark, I suspect it'll just be machinery and power."

"This level, then." Haldar stepped off the stairs and across the landing. Down the corridor he could see that, as well as the dim inbuilt light sources, it was also illuminated by the light coming through panels that made up the right hand wall. Each had a large transparent section which started perhaps two feet from the floor and finished just below the corridor ceiling. Quietly, he moved along the corridor, conscious of Bartan following him. At the first panel he stopped and peered carefully through the transparent plate. He ducked back. "It's a ward; they're getting people settled into it—a lot of women, men with guns, and lab-techs."

He dropped low to the ground and crawled past the panel, making sure he couldn't be seen from inside. Bartan followed him on hands and knees. At the second panel, Haldar stopped again and cautiously risked a glance.

"An operating theatre, empty." He knelt and took another, longer look. "Yes, empty, with lab-techs cleaning it.

Bartan joined him. "Automated operating booths as well, then."

"Not sure I would fancy going into one of them."

"They're OK if you set them up to just keep doing the same operation. Lock in the basic settings, check your parameters, leave a lab-tech in charge, and everything will be fine. Mostly."

Haldar made his way along the corridor to the next panel. "Medical stores, I'd say."

Bartan joined him. "These view-panels are part of a larger access panel; can we open them from this side?"

Haldar ran his fingers round the edge of the access panel. "No handles on this side, but at the bottom here you can see where the catch clips into the floor, holding the panel shut."

Bartan lay down for a closer view and whispered, "Got a knife?"

Haldar passed down a short utility knife and Bartan produced one of his own. Using one knife to lever the catch up, Bartan used the second to pin the catch in place while he repositioned the first knife to lever the catch a little more. Slowly, he managed to withdraw the catch. "Right, push gently."

Haldar did, and the bottom of the access panel swung into the store room. Bartan slid under the hatch. He grabbed the nearest box and pulled it towards him, jamming the panel open.

"Right, let's take a look."

Haldar crawled into the room and stood up. Bartan had already passed down a narrow aisle between two racks, and Haldar followed him. By the time he caught up, Bartan was rubbing the top of a cabinet with his glove. "Freezer cabinet; I'm trying to read the label." Bartan tried the handle and the freezer cabinet opened. He reached in and picked up the top container. He grunted and passed it to Haldar, who studied it carefully. The top was transparent, and inside he could see a honeycomb-like structure. Each cell in the 'honeycomb' held a small blob of tissue about half an inch across. What held his attention was the label. He read it aloud. "H/Sap exogenous ovaries. Pre-fertilised. Genotype 13/214/7B/Tsarina."

"Come across them before?" Bartan asked.

"I was trained in navel intelligence, not obstetrics."

Bartan collected his thoughts. "I've seen the brochures and I went on the 'familiarisation visits'. They're replacement ovaries. Each is pre-loaded with about a score of already fertilised eggs. At fixed intervals the ovary will release an egg, and at the same time, jump-start the whole endocrine process. You get annual pregnancy without all the time-wasting romance business."

"Who uses them?"

"Anyone who wants a set number of females to produce genetically-identical offspring; Grorin-Tech will tailor the genes for you. You want someone strong and docile suitable for fieldwork? Use these, and not only will the next generation be suitable, their offspring will pass on the desirable genetic traits. I've heard of them producing everything from dancing girls all the way down to their three-foot-tall maintenance humanoids."

"So they ship women in, fit these ovaries and ship them back out. Why go to the cost of shipping women?"

"Grorin-Tech are wary about who they allow to access their technology. I suspect that doing it this way keeps the costs up, and high cost allows for larger margins."

Haldar went to the freezer and looked at the other containers. "This one is Genotype 13/214/7B/Tsarina, this one Genotype 13/214/7F/Tsarina, and this one Genotype 13/214/7H/Tsarina."

Bartan looked pensive. "Difficult to tell, but I'd guess we have one basic Genotype, implanted on Tsarina, with a number of variants. Take some samples—it's probably cold enough outside to keep them viable for testing, if nothing else."

Haldar picked up a container from the floor. "Here's an empty one." He read the label. "Genotype 1a/Croton."

Bartan said, "Didn't Padro mention clients from Croton? Perhaps this was left from their job?"

The lights flashed twice and somewhere in the distance a siren sounded.

Haldar stuffed the containers into his pack and closed the freezer. "I wonder if that is about us. I think we might want to be out of here."

He made his way to the access panel and crawled out. Bartan followed him and kicked the box out of the way. The panel slowly closed and clicked shut. Bartan looked both ways down the corridor. "Which way now?"

Haldar pointed. "I think continue onwards, the way we were going; we should meet the staircase we came in on and we know what the ground is like above." Unslinging his rifle, he ran down the corridor, Bartan following. Haldar reached the stairwell and started running up the stairs. At the top, by the outer door, he halted, Bartan coming up behind him. Haldar said, "Right, our best bet is probably to bluff it out rather than fight. We're wearing Bar-Khan parkas; they might think we're local. Take your lead from me, and if it gets me killed, try something different." He opened the door and strode out. Muttering "I suppose it makes sense," Bartan followed him. Outside, the snow was heavier than it had been, and it was daylight. Bartan closed the doors behind them, glad to be out of the place at last. "What now?"

From off to the left, there were shouts and a group of figures ran through the snow, heading for the perimeter. The last figure obviously saw Haldar and Bartan. "What are you two standing there for? We have incoming. Move out and hold the perimeter, looking in. Move it!"

He turned and ran after the men he had been with. Haldar glanced at Bartan. "Well, you heard the man. Move it." He began to run towards the track they'd followed when they entered the village. Their course led them to the left of the other party, who were soon lost from visibility in the snow.

*****

Perhaps half a mile from the village, they stopped and Haldar picked a course away from the track. "We want to be outside the perimeter, if they're going to be firing inwards."

Bartan caught up with him. "Why inwards?"

Haldar pointed upwards. "There. Incoming ship. We'd have seen it earlier if it wasn't for the cloud base."

Bartan looked up. Above them was a spaceship, descending with alarming speed. "What is it?"

"Whatever it *was*, I'd guess it's been fitted out as an assault ship." Haldar looked round hurriedly. "Quick, over here; get among these rocks. Hopefully, they're too big to move."

They scrambled away from the path and halted in the cover of the rocks. Haldar hunkered down and gestured to Bartan to do likewise. "They're boulders, but hopefully they go down a long way. Shouldn't move too much if people start getting casual with explosives."

The ship was slowing rapidly; it was now barely a hundred feet up. It looked as if the captain intended to land at a level area next to the village. Haldar guessed it was perhaps two hundred feet long and fifty wide. There were a series of sharp 'crack' sounds as the two turrets, fore and aft, opened fire at positions on the hillside. Haldar crouched lower and closer to the rock. "They're probably just trying to keep any defenders' heads down; I don't think they'll have acquired any targets yet. The snow isn't going to help their targeting systems." Suddenly, from the hillside to their left, there was the sound of an explosion as a great bolt of energy flew through the snow and hit the ship. A pool of incandescence appeared on the hull and slowly faded. The ship shuddered, righted itself, and landed.

"What was that?" Bartan asked, his eyes closed; bright after-images were dancing in front of his eyes.

"It'll be the pulse laser." Harlan noticed that Bartan didn't seem to understand the significance of this comment, so elaborated, "They're using high-energy weapons in atmosphere. As the energy passes through the air, there is an explosion of superheated air and steam away from the line of fire. It takes a lot of energy, though, so the bolt does less damage when it hits."

The turrets had obviously spotted the pulse laser emplacement and were returning fire. The other pulse laser opened fire from the other side of the valley.

"How can the ship cope with this sort of attack?" Bartan asked as the ship rocked under the repeated hits.

"Energy dissipation; a high proportion of the energy in the bolt is used to boil off the snow and displace the air."

Now the ship hatches had opened, and infantry were storming out. Bulky figures in armour and helmets, they carried short, stubby weapons. Haldar suspected the ship would hold a reinforced company, perhaps a hundred and fifty men. He'd travelled on such ships and hated it; life was possible only because so many of the men travelled in sleeping berths, woken only occasionally to exercise and eat. It made for good assault infantry, since men would face pretty much anything rather than spend more time in the ship.

The infantry were met with a fusillade from the defenders: a few fell, others returned fire but kept on advancing, apparently intent on establishing their own perimeter. Then, in the upper hull of the ship, a panel slid back, revealing a missile rack. A score of missiles flew out, crossed the valley and exploded against the far rock face. One of the pulse lasers was silenced. "Good thinking; they've reprogrammed the anti-fighter defences." Haldar sounded almost paternal. "The weather won't really affect them."

The other pulse laser fell silent as another missile rack was revealed. As the missiles launched, the pulse laser fired six energy pulses in rapid succession. Bartan and Haldar both pressed themselves close to the ground, shielding their eyes. The air stank of ozone. The first pulse did little damage, but the succeeding pulses tore into the ship, ripping it open and setting it on fire. At the same time, the missiles struck the area of the pulse laser, and that one too fell silent.

Bartan licked his lips, the very air tasted burned. "So what happened there," he asked, his eyes still on the burning ship.

Haldar explained. "The gun commander drained his capacitors, probably damaged them irreparably, but by sending the bolts down the same path in quick succession, the first one cleared the way for the others. By the time the third one went down the path, it was probably passing through near vacuum."

Haldar had kept his attention on the fire-fight below. The burning ship was now being rocked by explosions as missile racks and volatile liquid stores 'cooked off'. From the mouth of the gorge, the defenders were mounting a counter-attack, which was making ground. Haldar noticed that a small knot of the infantry was slowly making its way towards the defended perimeter below where the last pulse laser had been. Haldar tried his phone and heard nothing but static. He turned to Bartan.

"We've got to get out of here and get up to the top of the ridge where we camped. There is too much ionisation down here for a signal. Keep low and let's get moving."

Not looking to see if he was being followed, Haldar, bent double, made his way at a crouching run. He dropped onto the track and kept running. He could hear Bartan behind him so didn't waste time by looking back. The snow had turned to rain—Haldar assumed this was a side effect of the energy battle. Behind them, he could hear the rattle of small arms fire. There seemed to be two separate actions, one around the burning ship and village, and another off to one side. He reached a bend in the track and took cover behind a rock.

He tried to keep his breathing shallow; the air tasted metallic, with the hint of something organic that irritated the back of the throat. Bartan caught up with him and dropped to the ground besides him. Haldar pulled his vision enhancer out and looked towards the sound of firing. Besides him, Bartan asked "I realise I'm just a cop who came along for the ride, but aren't things getting a bit out of hand?"

Haldar grinned as he surveyed the scene. "You've made it this far at a decent pace, you cannot be that unfit." He continued to scan the area. "We've got a small war going on down there, and I'm going to make it bigger. The arrival of the ship and its infantry is all the excuse I need to bring in support. I'm going to call in the military; they can end the fighting, and incidentally, let you and me investigate that lab facility at our leisure."

Bartan took a drink from his water bottle. "I joined as a beat cop, not a paramilitary. I'm excused warfare. I'm sure I've got a note from my mother somewhere, if it helps."

Haldar tried his phone again and muttered something. Then he turned to Bartan, "Keep that note handy, still far too much ionisation. Come on, we've got to get to the top of the ridge."

He set off up along the track at a fast jog. Bartan shrugged and followed. They covered another mile and Haldar stopped again. The fire-fight was still raging below. Haldar looked through the vision enhancer again. Bartan sank down behind a rock next to him. Bartan was vaguely comforted to discover that Haldar's breathing sounded as bad as his own. The self-confessed beat cop lay still and gradually felt his heart rate slow. Slowly, he rolled over onto one elbow and asked, "OK, what's happening? Only this time in slightly more detail."

Haldar continued to study the valley below them. Finally he said, "The bunch round the ship is going to be overrun, no doubt about it. The other group who are trying to cut their way out are still going. They've found a weak spot in the perimeter and they've made it weaker. They're heading towards the pulse laser position we passed earlier, and from there they might be able to get up the slope and away. We've got to get ahead of them; I want a word."

"Any particular word?"

"Well, 'Excuse me but what are you doing on my planet' will probably do for starters."

Haldar got to his feet again. "Come on, one last push. Last one to the top buys lunch."

"Provided it doesn't contain yak, it'll be a pleasure."

*****

Haldar sprawled behind a low rock and looked down the valley. Bartan, panting heavily, shrugged his pack off and lay on his back. He worked the bolt on his rifle, loading a round into the breech before rolling back onto his stomach. "Who are you going to call first, the restaurant or the military?"

Haldar pulled out his phone and checked. "At last, I've got a signal. No wonder these satellite phones haven't caught on." Hastily, he punched in some numbers and waited. Bartan moved a couple of stones that were digging into him and watched. Haldar gave him a thumbs-up then spoke into the phone.

"Haldar Drom here; put me through to the Colonel, please." There was a pause, then Bartan heard Haldar say, "I couldn't care less, just put me through!"

There was another pause and Haldar's tone changed. "Look Marine, I don't care if you have to shoot his mistress to attract his attention, I want him on this phone now!" Haldar glanced at Bartan and rolled his eyes. Suddenly his attention went back to the phone. "Aled, that you?" Whatever Aled was about to say was brutally cut off. "No time, Aled, have you got a couple of spare battalions?" ... "Well, what about the battalion on standby in the suborbitals?" Silence again. "Well, I've got a cosy little infantry battle going on down here, with one assault ship in flames; I think it trumps 'unconfirmed reports'." Haldar listened and then broke the connection.

"Now we wait for him to decide what to do next."

Before Bartan could comment, the phone rang. This time, Haldar pressed the loud speaker button and glanced at Bartan, "You might as well listen."

"Haldar here."

"Hi Haldar; Jonno here. The Colonel told me you've got problems. What do you want my boys to do?"

Haldar glanced down the valley. "Lock in on my phone, that'll give you a position. I'm on a ridge overlooking the valley. Can you see it on your map display?"

There was a pause, and then the voice came back. "Yes, got it."

"Well, drop one of your suborbitals with us, one on the other side of the valley, one at the outlet end of the gorge to stop them running that way, and perhaps the fourth as a reserve."

"Will do; be with you in an hour. Can you keep yourself out of trouble that long?"

"We'll try. Basically there is one small group trying to cut its way out in my direction. I hope to rescue them and keep them for questioning. However, there are a lot of heavily armed locals, and a major unlicensed medical facility down there that needs dealing with; I'm hoping your lads will encourage a general mood of good will and an urge to cooperate with the authorities."

"Do I detect the unspoken 'without doing too much damage'?"

Haldar paused briefly. "Most of the medical facility seems to be below ground, so is probably safe from light weapons. However if you'd been intending to use major naval support, I'd like to discourage you now."

There was a laugh from the other end of the phone. "I know, when there's anything delicate, call in the marines. See you in an hour."

Haldar broke the connection. "Now to see what our friends below are up to."

Bartan peered round a rock. "I think they've reached the place where the pulse laser was installed."

Haldar crawled forward and looked through his vision enhancer. "The emplacement looks to have been converted into molten slag, but they'll still get some cover in the track behind it."

Bartan said, "Look right, there are some locals trying to get round their flank."

Haldar looked where Bartan was pointing and made his decision. "You any good with that rifle you've been lugging about for the last week?"

Bartan nodded. "I got basic marksman."

"Right, you keep them pinned down, and I'll go and have a chat with our friends from the assault ship."

*****

Haldar picked up his rifle and made his way down the slope, moving from boulder to boulder. He got to within twenty yards of the destroyed bunker and stopped. He had given some thought to his approach and had decided to use 'Ship talk.' This dialect had spread through ports and merchant ships and had been picked up by many naval forces as well.

"Hey, you boys! You want out?"

There was silence, and then someone shouted back.

"Who you?"

"Haldar Drom, Tsarina intel."

"What you want?"

"Talk."

Behind him, he could hear the crack of Bartan's rifle.

"Who shoot?"

"I got cover. Keep heads down. They flank you if we chitter."

There was silence again. He suspected they were discussing the situation. Then there was another shout.

"What talk?"

"Who hire you? What you do here?"

There was that silence again, so Haldar added, "I can keep you live."

Behind him, Bartan fired twice in quick succession and then a third shot.

"Haste or we stuck."

Obviously a decision had been reached. "We move."

"Up to top of hill, come with me."

Haldar started to work his way back up the hill, trying to keep in cover as he did so. As he glanced behind him, eight men had suddenly burst out of the cover and were making their way up the slope. They seemed competent—half would run, the other half would be in firing positions. Then the runners would halt, take up position and the other men would run past them and further up the hill. Bartan's rifle cracked again, and Haldar looked north. He could see a group of men mustering in cover. He rested his rifle on the rock and took careful aim. In the sparse grass ahead of him, a tiny cherry red beetle was climbing up a stem. As Haldar watched, it seemed to be reaching out to clamber from one stem to another. Suddenly, where he was aiming, two men ran out from behind the cover while the others fired wildly in the direction of Bartan. Haldar fixed the sights on the runner in the lead and fired. The rifle slammed into his shoulder, but the kick wasn't has hard as he'd half remembered. The man jerked back as if he'd been hit by a thrown rock and spun round. The second man dove for cover. Haldar frantically worked the bolt, slamming another round into the breech. He looked downhill; the surviving infantry were almost up with him. One dropped behind the same rock as him, took up a firing position and said "Go."

Haldar sprinted up the slope. From behind him came a sound like ripping silk, someone was laying down covering fire. He breasted the rise and threw himself down behind a rock. He peered round it and ducked back as something ricocheted of it, inches from his face. He wiped grit off his face and risked another look. He could see more men in Bar-Khan parkas working their way round the right flank, partially concealed by low scrub and loose boulders. Haldar took careful aim and fired. A man went down, but Haldar assumed he had dived for cover rather than been hit. As he worked the bolt again, Haldar noticed blood smeared on the back of his right hand. He dabbed his face again, some of the grit had cut his cheek. He now had the taste of blood on his tongue when he licked his lips. He ignored it and carefully aimed the rifle at where he had last seen the enemy.

As the first infantrymen scrambled up the slope in front of him and took cover among the rocks on both sides of him, Haldar fired eight shots in swift succession. He had no target, but he could encourage the enemy to keep their heads down. Bartan's rifle cracked again, and Haldar assumed that Bartan could see targets he couldn't. Then the rest of the infantry arrived and spread themselves out further along the ridge. Haldar ducked behind his rock to reload the magazine, and gave his attention to his new companions. Each man carried a firearm Haldar didn't recognise. They wore thermoplastic carapace armour with back and breast plates, arm and leg plates, and a helmet with a visor which Haldar assumed would have integral head-up display. The armour had a nondescript camouflage pattern, and under the armour the men wore plain fatigues.

They struck him as both calm and capable, and the fact they were alive at all confirmed this. He noticed one man crawling towards him. This one was different; Haldar couldn't quite put his finger on it, but he seemed to have been hastily equipped with pieces of armour that almost fitted, and no one had had the time to mould them to fit perfectly. Also, the man was carrying a locally-made rifle similar to Haldar's own.

Pulling himself along with his elbows, the man joined Haldar behind his rock. He lifted his helmet visor and Haldar could see the man was middle aged with a thin face and a reasonable tan. The man stretched out his hand. "I'm Toulis Hart. I'm a loss adjuster for Trans-world (Tsarina) Insurance."

Haldar took his hand, and glanced pointedly down into the valley. "If it's any help, my professional opinion is that your ship is a write-off."

Toulis laid his rifle down and reached into a pocket. This involved him fishing about under the armour, which to Haldar was absolute proof that he was wearing something cobbled together from whatever was left in the company store. He produced a business card which read 'Toulis Hart. Trans-world (Tsarina) Insurance. Your first port of call for goods in transit, merchant vessels of all sorts and every type of warehousing facility. Assuring you of our personal attention at all times.' This was followed by a Kaunas City address and a phone number.

Haldar put the card into his wallet. "I'm Haldar Drom of the Governor's Investigation Office." He gestured round. "So, what exactly is going on and why have you started a war on my nice, quiet planet?"

Toulis pulled himself up and sat next to Haldar, his back to the rock. "Simple. Does the name of Wayland Strang mean anything to you?" Before Haldar could comment Toulis added, "Obviously, I don't want to get into legal arguments here, but Mr Strang has considerable legitimate business interests, including Trans-world (Tsarina) Insurance. As his legitimate representative on Tsarina, I'm investigating a threat to his interests."

"With a bluidy infantry company to carry your briefcase?"

Toulis sighed. "Mr Strang was worried that my investigation might be thwarted by local criminal elements. Me, I just thought that it would be nice to have company, and these gentlemen came within budget."

Haldar turned to face the loss adjuster. "Look, life is going to be so much easier if we just put our cards on the table and be honest with each other."

Toulis looked a little surprised. "As a gambit, it has the advantage of novelty." He adjusted his body armour to try and get it comfortable. "Oh, what the hell; try anything once."

Haldar grinned. "Right, I have a marine battalion on its way, I expect it in less than half an hour. Therefore we have an excellent chance of living through this episode." Off to one side he heard the crack of Bartan's rifle, and then two short controlled bursts as one of the infantry fired. Bartan called out. "Sorry about that, Haldar, some of them had got a bit close."

Haldar turned back to Toulis. "Might have to downgrade the 'excellent'. Anyway, I'm here to see what they are doing down there in the valley, and from my point of view it sounds like bad news. Why are you here? Has Mr Strang got too much money tied up in the production of Abate?"

There was a brief silence, and then Toulis said "yes." Again he adjusted the poorly fitting armour. "This whole honesty idea isn't making things any easier. Yes, Strang wanted the labs shut down, but he had been hearing rumours of Grorin-Tech involvement that went over and above just making pharmaceuticals."

"They seem to be running a pre-fertilised ovary implant service."

Toulis grimaced. "That isn't good."

"Well, I wasn't impressed, but I might just be old fashioned," Haldar said dryly.

His phone rang and he answered it. "Haldar Drom."

The voice on the other end said "Jonno here. You still OK?"

"There are unpleasant people getting closer, but I think we're holding them off."

"Right, we'll be over you in about five minutes. I've dropped a mortar section off. They'll put down a barrage in front of you; how far in front?"

Haldar peered round the rock. "How good are your boys?"

"Plus or minus ten yards."

"Go for sixty yards beyond us. Just make sure they get my position marked accurately."

"No worries; see you in about five minutes." The connection was cut and the phone went quiet.

Haldar turned to Toulis. "Five minutes and we'll have marines."

"Good. And when they take the village down there, can I come with you and look at the Grorin-Tech material?"

Above, Haldar heard a whine. He shouted "Heads down, everyone!" and rolled over to his front. Seconds later, there was a series of explosions down the slope in front of them. Haldar's phone rang and he answered it.

"Jonno here; how was that?"

"Well, it didn't hit us, which is a good start."

"I'll have the lads walk the barrage at ten yards a round." The connection went dead. Haldar could now hear the suborbital, somewhere behind them.

"Mortars?" Toulis couldn't have sounded more surprised if the marines had arrived carrying flint axes.

"Mortars" Haldar confirmed. "They're so cheap you wouldn't believe, immune to most forms of countermeasures, and man-portable at a push."

"Surely any decent point defence system can take them out?"

"Absolutely," Haldar grinned. "A hundred-credit mortar can keep a ten-thousand-credit point defence system amused all day."

The suborbital was coming in above them now; its hatches already open and the landing ramps dropping even as the craft made the last fifty yards of its descent.

"The mortars have stopped."

Haldar grinned. "It's all a matter of trajectories, Toulis. It's embarrassing if you shoot down your own air support."

As if on cue, the explosions started up again further down the slope. Marines fanned out down the ramps, securing a perimeter, and then started moving across to join the firing line. Haldar could see that on the other side of the valley a second suborbital was landing.

"Toulis, you and I can get out of the way now, and you'd better get your men to join us, I think they can stand down now."

Haldar raised himself into a half crouch and sprinted back towards the approaching marines. He purposefully kept his rifle slung just in case anyone was nervous. Toulis followed him, shouting for his infantry. Haldar glanced back, checking that Bartan was following them. Haldar halted in a depression and the others joined him. He ran his eyes over the infantry, and noticed one had some sort of insignia. Haldar tapped his arm. "You boss?"

The infantryman snapped a salute. "Sarge."

Haldar pointed to the marines who were moving cautiously past them. "You give them sit-rep. Show where indigs are."

The sergeant jogged off to join the marines; Haldar could see him talking to the Lieutenant and making sweeping gestures with his right arm. He turned his attention back to Toulis, who had joined him.

"Right, so when the marines have cleared the area, you want to join us checking things out."

Toulis replied sharply. "Yes."

"So what are you looking for, exactly?"

Toulis allowed his glance to fall on the infantry clustering round them. "That is perhaps an answer for another time and place."

"Fair enough, try this one. Who are these infantry, exactly?"

Toulis turned to the man nearest him. "You give him the details; don't stick to ship talk."

"Third Independent Assault Company, Finswallow Brigade, sir."

"A mercenary formation?"

"Yes sir, we tend to work a lot further in, towards the Galactic Centre, sir."

"And what brought you so far out?"

"Money, sir," answered the soldier, smartly.

Haldar turned to Toulis. "So why doesn't Mr Strang use his own men, or is that another question for another time and place?"

Toulis had the grace to smile. "I'd be grateful, yes."

Haldar glanced round in the direction of the valley. There was a brisk fire-fight going on and mortar rounds were still falling. The sergeant was making his way back. Haldar waited for the man to re-join them, then turned to look at the mercenaries said, "I think it is time to discuss your future, gentlemen."

They eyed him warily, but no one said anything. He continued, "As far as I can see, your contract was not with Tsarina. Therefore, I don't think there are any repatriation conditions we have to stick to." He paused here and studied them. "Your employer may not wish you any harm, but I cannot imagine he will hasten to ransom you." Haldar looked at Toulis, who sighed.

"If it is any consolation, I don't think he'll hasten to ransom me, either."

"Right," here Haldar's tone switched from didactic to decisive. "This is the deal. Both our navy and marines accept 'Out-system Volunteers'. Normally, men sign on for five years or longer. As far as I can tell, no one out there is particularly bothered about helping you." Haldar counted his points off on his fingers. "You're unlikely to be able to pay your own passage home, so if you spontaneously volunteer for five years in the Marines, I'll be so overwhelmed by this evidence of your good intentions that I'll be bound to recommend that the Marines accept you. You'd serve five years, same terms and conditions as everyone else, with your papers made out in whatever name and details you give them. Then in five years' time, you are a citizen, and can reapply for another term, leave the military and get a job, or even travel off-world, as every Tsarina citizen is entitled to do."

The sergeant stepped forward. "Keen to apply to be an Out-system Volunteer, sir." Behind him, the other men added their own requests.

Haldar relaxed slightly. "Welcome aboard, we'll go over to the ship and get you boys sworn in. One last thing; if any of you have dependents that you want to join you, tell the man when you sign on. There is a loan scheme set against your pay, which will allow them to join you."

As Haldar led the party out of the depression, there was the sound of a large explosion behind them, and the ground quivered under their feet. Haldar picked himself up, having thrown himself instinctively to the ground. He sprinted to towards the edge of the ridge and looked down into the valley. Where the village had been was a raging fire, the flames burning with hints of green and blue. Haldar's phone rang. He clicked it on.

"It wasn't my boys," said Jonno's voice.

"You sure someone didn't get a bit over enthusiastic with the support?"

"Haldar, you know as well as I do that there is a limit to what you can achieve with light support weapons. Anyway, we've not even engaged the village yet."

"Thanks Jonno, keep me posted anyway." Haldar broke the connection. He turned to Toulis, who had caught up with him.

"Well, it isn't anything to do with us," he said, noting Haldar's questioning look. "Our heavy kit burned with the ship, we lost our demolition charges."

Haldar turned to Bartan. Before he could say anything Bartan said "Just as a matter of record, the New Charity Gendarmerie disclaim any responsibility for the incident." He grinned. "Probably kids playing with matches."

Haldar sighed. "It's going to make investigating things tricky. I don't think we'll get far poking the ashes with a stick."

Chapter 4

As the tides flow through the Straits of Farrant, they create a maelstrom of spectacular size and power. This has been a popular tourist destination, and people would stay in Raterton and travel out to view it from the shore or take a flitter trip over it. But because of an accident of geography, Farrant Point not only funnels the waters which create the maelstrom, but also on its lee side protects a large stretch of coast line stretching west as far as the Colitas Delta. This area, rich in fishing villages better known for their picturesque decay than their diligence, stretches from Kaunas City to the fading resort town of Raterton at the foot of the Farrant point.

In Raterton itself, the accent is still on faded gentility rather than poverty and neglect. Squamous reptilian Sea Dragons, two feet long, may forage the bins, contesting their contents with stray dogs and feral cats, but they do so after dark. Similarly, even the empty properties on the sea front have their curtains drawn back each morning and closed each evening by proprietors from neighbouring guesthouses. Drifters and down-and-outs scour the storm wrack on the beach for tampsi and coalbladder, which they sell to cooks or tourists. They know better than to refuse the offer of a wash, a shave or a hair cut from the town's matriarchs, who have established a discrete salon for just this purpose.

The wavedivers, four-winged reptilian fish eaters, are considered quaint, and thus are allowed to perch on the statues of town worthies which plague the promenade. The crockadil beetles, which gather wavediver dung into huge stinking balls as nurseries for their noisome young, are not. Thus the town pays a small retainer, which enables an elderly mendicant of uncertain religious adherence to live with charming abstinence in a grotto at the unfashionable end of the sea front, in return for keeping it swept clean.

This was the town where Bartan and Toulis sat in the bar of a small hotel, making uncomfortable small-talk as they waited for Haldar. When they arrived back at Kaunas City, Haldar had put them into a taxi, given the driver directions, and told them to wait for him there. The taxi had taken them out along the coast, past a string of villas and the occasional fishing village, until it had arrived at a small town the driver had dismissed as 'Raterton.' He'd found the hotel for them and abandoned them at the front door. Bartan had thought the taxi driver's departure had been a bit brusque until Toulis pointed out that he'd been paid using a voucher from the Governor's Private Office. The two men wandered into the hotel, to be met by a young man on reception who was expecting them, and led them upstairs to their rooms. Bartan took an immediate liking to his. The room was large, timber panelled and each of the ceiling beams was cut from a different sort of timber. The furniture was also wood, well-worn but cared for. They had agreed to meet in the bar after taking the opportunity to wash and change, and now were both rather regretting not setting the rendezvous time a little later.

The receptionist, who proved also to be the barman, had recommended a local beer, and the two men nursed glass tankards. So far, the only topic of conversation that presented no problems was that the beer was something of an acquired taste.

Eventually Bartan emptied his tankard and put it down on the table.

"Toulis, we have a problem here. I am a policeman, through and through; equally, you obviously aren't. But what are you?"

Toulis sighed. "Seriously, I really am a loss adjuster." He ignored Bartan's look of disbelief. "I started off serving a term in the navy, mainly in engineering, and then when I left the service loss adjusting was just something I drifted into. Anyway, I worked for a firm that was taken over by Trans-world Insurance, and we got the (Tsarina) stuck in the middle of it. On some planets, loss adjusters are not supposed to be part of the same company as insurers, but on Tsarina the regulations aren't all that tightly drawn. Anyway, just out of personal interest I delved a bit into Trans-world, and discovered that its major shareholder was a Starmancer. So I watched and waited. From my point of view, my reports went in as usual, and if anything the money was paid out faster than before. Anyway, about ten years ago, I was summoned to Havadon to the company HQ. There I was told, very firmly, that I was engaged in a legitimate business, and it was to stay scrupulously legitimate. That was fine by me; from my experience our current owner, smuggler, pirate, or to use the more popular term, Starmancer, was running a more ethical business than the people he'd bought the company off."

Bartan interrupted. "I can see how you drifted into it, but how come you end up with a mercenary company 'investigating' a drug lab?"

Toulis swirled the beer round. "I could hear the inverted commas." He took a drink from his tankard. "Simple. To an extent my job involved investigation, since insurance companies do face a lot of fraud. I think I'm pretty good at my job, and perhaps other people do, because five years ago I was called to Havadon again and given another investigation to carry out that wasn't insurance related. Since then, I've been engaged in 'policing' the legitimate arm of a criminal organisation." Toulis looked out of the window for a while. "If we're being honest, I suppose I was bored. Yes, my job can occasionally be interesting, but exciting? Not a hope." He gave a tired smile. "It's funny, talking to you and Haldar; you're both so much alike, both driven by something, both policemen to the core of your being. I'd struggle to imagine you doing anything else. Me, I enjoyed the navy, but didn't fit in well enough for them to offer me a further term of enlistment. I suppose I jumped into working for Wayland Strang because the job held out the hope of excitement. The lab is an example of it. Yes, I was just 'the man on the spot', and if I'd asked, they'd have sent in a professional to lead the assault. But it was my chance to do something more interesting that accountancy. That being said, I did some research. It was then I discovered that if you used the correct transponder code, you didn't get picked up by the satellites."

"How did you come across that one?"

Toulis smiled. "When people know you're connected with Mr Strang, all sorts of interesting individuals come out of the woodwork trying to sell you things." His tone became more serious. "I put together what I could find out, but most of the evidence came from off-planet. Eventually, I was called to a rendezvous out-of-system and told that Mr Strang himself had taken the decision that the lab was to be closed down, and that I was asked to go in with the assault team to check out what was happening there. I was told that it wasn't just drugs."

Bartan nodded. "But why an infantry assault?

"I can only assume that Strang knew about the level of security; but more than that, he was desperate to find out what is—or rather, what *was* going on."

"So what does Mr Strang think was going on?"

Toulis was silent for a while. "I wasn't told, as such. In fact they weren't going to tell me at all, but I pointed out that it is difficult to investigate when you don't have motives and suchlike. In the end, the executive who was briefing me went out to contact someone and another chap came in, one of Strang's friends."

Bartan raised an eyebrow, a technique he'd mastered early in his police career. "Friends?"

"Strang is an enigma. Now, only his friends ever meet him. Some years ago he was a swashbuckling pirate, the classic Starmancer. Now he rarely meets people. Whether he's paranoid or whether he's trying to create an air of mystery, I don't know. What he does have is a handful of people he trusts absolutely. They're known as his friends. Given difficulties of communication, where nothing moves faster than a spaceship, you need men you can trust, who can make decisions with full authority and not have to refer everything to the boss. The friends are the people he trusts to do this. This particular friend had taken on this case. Basically, he told me that they are worried that Grorin-Tech had gotten hold of some of Mr Strang's DNA. If true, it wasn't good news."

There was silence as Bartan appeared to digest the information, and Toulis asked, "So how did you get into the job? Have you always been in the police?"

Bartan stood up and took the tankards to the bar. The barman was reading a magazine of some sort—Bartan could see the pictures, mainly of boats and engines. The barman wordlessly put down his magazine and refilled the two tankards. He picked up the magazine again and continued reading; Bartan took the tankards back to the table.

"I thought you might need something first."

Toulis looked taken aback. "Why, were you a Starmancer or something before becoming a policeman?"

"Worse than that, even; I was a musician."

"Professional?" Toulis's tone changed. The world-weary air was still there, but there was something else, a touch of enthusiasm perhaps.

Bartan stared ruefully into his tankard. "Well, I survived for nearly two years, but the second winter I just about starved to death. I was reduced to busking near a freight terminal in the hope I could get the money for a ride home. An old gendarmerie sergeant saw me, felt sorry for me and arrested me for loitering so that he could take me back to the station and feed me. I played him and the others there a tune or two, and next morning, as he let me out, he asked me if I had any real plans. I hadn't, so he offered me a job." Bartan's voice was soft, almost as if he was getting lost in the memory. "At least I knew the food was good."

Bartan leaned back in his seat. "Funny really, I haven't thought of it for years. Yet, on Tsarina this is the second time those particular memories have come back."

"Second time?" Toulis asked.

"Sorry, I forgot you weren't there. The first time was in Purity, at Padro's Place. That was when I heard Kollette sing. My best times were when I was travelling with a girl who had a good voice."

"What did you play?" Even as he heard it, Bartan could sense a hesitation in Toulis's voice.

"Nine-string starcaster." Bartan kept his voice casual.

"Ever try a seven-string?"

"Yes. Loved the chords, but somehow it couldn't carry the melody. Also, I just loved the two necks of the nine-string."

Toulis seemed to come to a decision. He looked across to the bar and attracted the barman's attention. "Is there a shop selling musical instruments in town?"

"Certainly sir, old Musgrave sells most things. Makes a fair few of them, as well."

"Will he be open?"

"Not sure if I've ever known him shut, not while he's awake anyway."

Toulis turned to Bartan. "Drink your beer, we're going out. It's years since I played the seven-string, and it's about time I took it up again."

*****

Haldar arrived at Musgrave's music shop late. The door opened when he pushed it, and the lights were still on. Sitting on a table was Bartan, the fingers of his left hand dancing across the frets of a nine-string, while with his right hand he picked and coaxed the strings. Toulis sat in a chair opposite him, playing a simple pattern of chord sequences on a seven-string. As they played, a girl, perhaps fourteen, sang an old song about a lover who'd run off to become a Starmancer, promising to return to marry her when he had made good. An elderly man, whom Haldar recognized as Musgrave, was standing, quietly listening, as were four others of widely different ages. The song came to an end, the girl's voice fading away, and the two starcasters were silenced.

Bartan looked up. "Haldar, your Starmancer can play."

Toulis sniffed. "You never learned fingering like that in the police." He turned to the girl. "And thank you Kyl! If you decide to go professional, and need two broken-down elderly backing musicians, I'm sure we'll both leap arthritically at the opportunity."

Haldar said "I see you gentlemen managed to keep yourselves amused. Now, are you ready for a something to eat?"

"Do you play an instrument?" Toulis asked. "We could do with someone in percussion, perhaps chimes, or even a xylophone."

"Not really. Anyway, I was brought up with louder music with a faster driving beat. I was once told that starcasters are like bank managers; if they're not screaming, you're not playing them right. "

Toulis played a few harsh chords and said "I've not heard the expression, but it tells you everything you need to know about life."

"Not quite, otherwise on my wedding day it should have told me, 'Haldar Drom, do not marry this woman!'" Haldar turned to Musgrave. "Have you managed to get any money out of them?"

The old man shook his head. "Not yet, but you never know. They've started dreaming again, and who knows where that will take them."

"Busking on a dark winter's night, wondering whether I'll freeze or starve," Bartan said dolefully. He gently put the nine-string down on the desk. "But she's a beautiful instrument."

*****

Haldar led the other two out onto the pavement. Old Musgrave closed the door behind them.

Haldar led them down the alley back to the promenade. "You ever been to Raterton before, Toulis?"

"Yes, I've got a home in a fishing village between here and Kaunas City."

Haldar waved his arm down the promenade. "Born and brought up here; used to be a busy little town. When I was a kid it was thriving. We even had off-world tourists here for the maelstrom and the fishing; quite a lot of off-world trade. Along this street, the shops sold all sorts of stuff." He appeared to shrink into himself. "Now, look at it. There are at least sixteen shops or guesthouses empty. Three of the shops are pawnbrokers, and the rest are the sort that wouldn't have been able to afford the rents back then."

"So what went wrong?" Bartan asked.

Toulis said "I think I can guess. You don't get the visitors anymore."

"That's right. Here you see it more. In Kaunas City, the centre is still thriving, even if the outer suburbs have got a bit drear. But back then we used to call ourselves 'the edge of the universe'. There was some tourism, some trade. We're a peaceful, law-abiding sort of place really, even if we do have a pathological loathing of record keeping." He winked at Bartan. Then he turned to Toulis. "What are the insurance premiums on merchant shipping like now?"

"I know what you mean. Ironically, even Strang's merchant shipping pays the same price as everyone else. He may be a Starmancer, but he's just one more in a competitive market. I could name four or five who are dogging his heels and targeting his ships. They would happily break up his organisation in the hope they'd get some of the good bits."

"We're sliding slowly into the darkness again," Haldar said. "No obvious barbarians, no fall of empire, no great historical pageant. We're just drifting slowly, gently, into decline."

"And you're going to stop the rot?" Bartan asked.

Haldar stared out across the promenade. In the silence, they could hear waves stirring the gravel of the beach. When Haldar spoke his voice was soft, and they had to strain to hear. "Well, if I don't, who will? Someone has to do something, and I'm not prepared to sit and watch as the lights slowly go out." He fiddled with a bracelet on his right wrist. "Remember 'George'? Corruption gets into a society; it's like a disease, rotting the body from within." He walked across the promenade and stood, leaning on the railing, looking out to sea. Toulis and Bartan glanced at each other and followed him. Haldar ignored them but kept talking; they could plainly hear the anger and bitterness in his voice.

"I knew George. He had a wife and two children. Nice family, a Navy family. When he was court-martialled and disgraced, his wife couldn't face it and took a drugs overdose."

"The children?" Toulis asked.

"I assume George got them away with him when he disappeared."

"When we were talking with George, you mentioned an Investigating Officer." Bartan said. "I rather assumed from the way you were talking that it was you."

Haldar stared out over the sea, the light from the town caught the crests of the waves, bejewelling them as they broke. Out to sea small four-winged lizards dived for fish. Haldar watched them a while in silence. When he spoke the anger had faded, only the bitterness remained.

"Yes, I was the investigating officer. I had three warnings; the first was a quiet hint from another officer who said he'd heard rumours that I was upsetting people by asking too many questions. The second came from Doran himself; he was very tactful, but firm. The final warning came from my wife. She explained that her family were worried the family good name might be dragged through the dirt. Her brother was the Executive Officer on the Taurus, and George's immediate superior office."

"Your *wife?*" Toulis said, surprise evident in his voice.

"My soon to be ex-wife," Haldar confirmed. "She didn't want to be hitched to a loser."

He pulled himself upright. "It has to be said that the Investigations Office is considered a career dead end. But believe it or not, the Governor is a nice guy. I genuinely like him. He believes in justice, and is willing to bend the rules so that justice can happen." He turned to face them and the two men could see that the bitterness and anger had drained away. "Indeed, I'd probably keep doing the job, even if they stopped paying me." He paused and grinned, "But for gods' sake, don't tell the Governor that."

He led them past shuttered shops until he came to where light spilled out into the street. "Gentlemen, the Raterton Grill; the best food in Raterton, even if it is owned by a cousin of mine. It's somewhere we can talk, if only because I installed the surveillance suite myself."

He led them into the half-empty restaurant and took a table in a quiet alcove. The three men seated themselves, and Toulis looked around for a menu. "No menu," Haldar explained, "It's a set meal, different every day."

As if in response to his words, a waiter appeared, poured them each a glass of wine, and then retired. Toulis sipped, and nodded. "A pleasant white." He sniffed, "A moscato, at least in lineage. It shows both concentration and at least moderate complexity, while the notes of rich yellow fruits and spice are excellent, if perhaps lacking subtlety."

Bartan met Haldar's eye. "There are times when it becomes distressingly obvious whose organisation pays the best expenses."

"I'm afraid that I rarely manage better than stewed yak and beans in indeterminate sauce," Haldar added, with sad mock-pomposity. "Still, it behoves us to remember that we do occupy the moral high ground, and can at least maintain an air of smug self-congratulation."

They were spared Toulis's reply by the arrival of the soup course. The waiter placed a full bowl in front of each man, and a bowl of spiced crackers in the middle of the table, bowed and left.

Bartan picked up his bowl and sipped his soup from it. "Tasty, and not too hot."

Haldar watched him, somewhat askance, his own spoon poised. "Local food is spiced, but it isn't as hot as some." He dunked a cracker in his soup and ate it. "Still, we have an investigation to discuss. I think Bartan can go home and write up a success. The lab that was producing Abate has been comprehensively eliminated. Kenehan Independent Traders are still out there somewhere, but they'll have no more Abate to export."

"What was it that did the eliminating?" Toulis asked.

"Preliminary marine investigations suggest a self-destruct mechanism, perhaps fired remotely. Once it exploded, the defenders rather lost heart and tried to make a run for it. The marines say that we have to assume some got out—they knew the terrain, the marines didn't."

"Any sign of the Watch Company?" Bartan asked.

"No hard evidence. Some of the bodies were clean shaven, but were wearing local clothing. The two pulse laser positions had been seriously damaged, but there are investigators working through the ruins."

"Your office has a forensics department?" Bartan asked, his tone gently teasing.

Haldar had the grace to look slightly embarrassed. "Well, no, not as such. But I've got a friend in the university archaeology department, and he's set it as a project for a group of his more competent students, working under his supervision." Haldar changed the subject. "We're checking serial numbers on some captured weaponry, but I suspect they'll turn up some anonymous buyer."

The three men returned their attention to the soup, and then Haldar said, "However, from the point of view of the Governor, the arrival of the mercenaries is considered fortuitous."

"Fortuitous?" Toulis asked.

"Well, an exact quote would be 'damned lucky.' It gave me the perfect excuse to deploy marines and close the facility down, and the self-destruction eliminated any evidence, which means there will be no need for political embarrassment in the Border Kingdoms, or in the Governor's Office."

"So what happens next?"

"Well, we still have some samples that Bartan and I took."

"Samples?"

Haldar and Bartan recounted the tale of their exploits before the mercenaries had landed. The soup was finished and bowls were pushed to one side.

"A nice soup," Bartan said, mopping his lips with the napkin. "What was it?"

"Sheep's tripe and sliced intestines, cut fine, steamed and then cooked with ginger, chilli, and three or four other local sauces."

"Remind me not to ask next time."

"Back to these samples," Toulis said, his tone perhaps too casual, "What do they tell you?"

"Very little of importance," Haldar admitted. "Yes, we can get DNA sequences, but we don't know whose DNA it is, or what the sequences mean; not without growing an embryo."

Toulis said quietly, "My principal would really want to know about those embryos."

"I understand that, and my superiors do as well. Also, whatever happened happened on my watch, so I want to know what has been going on."

The waiter arrived and cleared the table. Then he deftly served them and withdrew. Bartan looked at his plate. "Sliced meat and vegetable on a bed of rice?"

"Don't worry, it isn't yak. I wouldn't do that to you."

Toulis tried some of the meat. "A 'white' meat, but it carries the flavour of the spices and vegetables well."

Haldar smiled proudly. "A local delicacy, we call it the traan. It's a squid-like creature which is stuffed with the vegetables and spices and is then steamed for some time to both cook it and leave it tender."

Bartan shrugged. "I'm beyond worrying. As you say, it isn't yak."

Haldar turned to Toulis. "We have the embryos in store, but we're stumped as to how to go further without allowing them to develop. To do that, we'd have to implant them and allow them to come to term naturally, and we're not keen on having some poor woman giving birth to gods alone know what."

Bartan put down his fork. "Why not ask Grorin-Tech? They will have records. We've got the genotype numbers."

Haldar asked, "And where do we get hold of Grorin-Tech?"

"That, I can help you with; they have representation at the permanent trade fair at the Havadon Higher Orbital Facility."

Toulis nodded. "Yes, I've been there. It is where the liners stop to take on passengers. The Facility is designed to save ships the cost of landing on a planet, going into atmosphere and then having to escape a planet's gravity-well when they try to leave."

The waiter appeared with another bottle of wine. This one he left, and departed silently. Haldar poured and asked, “I assume that you would be interested in travelling with me to Havadon?”

Toulis nodded. “Indeed.”

Bartan added. “I have to go there anyway, to change for New Charity. I’d like to tag along.”

Haldar sipped his wine. “Good.” He turned to Toulis. “But what exactly is going on with Strang’s organisation? Something is happening.”

“I’m not in the inner circle. I’m just someone they trust to investigate.” Toulis drained his glass. “But as I was saying, there is no shortage of competition in the world of the Starmancer. New leaders appear on the scene, get the breaks and become important, or disappear without trace when a navy catches them or one of their rivals mounts a successful assassination. Their captains watch them, constantly readying themselves to navigate the best course for themselves through the chaos if their leader falls, but at the same time, serving loyally in case he remains lucky and successful.”

Bartan swallowed some squid and said, “Sounds like office politics everywhere.”

“Yes, but the captains and the rest of the organisation are very sensitive to hints that their leader is losing it. A leader who fails in some plan or project will lose ships and men. Bolder spirits will try and go it alone; the more cautious will move to join the fleet of a competitor.”

“So it can be a self-fulfilling prophecy then,” Bartan said. “If you look weak, men will desert and you will become weak.”

Toulis nodded. “So as you can imagine, Wayland Strang is keen to get to the bottom of this episode, and if necessary, he must be seen to win. Can you imagine the damage it would do if it came out that a rival had used his DNA to produce field-workers? About five years ago one of Mr Strang’s senior people deserted the organisation. He just disappeared, along with a substantial amount of money, and no one has been able to find him. What is particularly worrying for Mr Strang is that this individual may have had access to Mr Strang’s DNA and medical contact details.”

“Would Grorin-Tech get involved in this sort of work?” Haldar asked Bartan.

Bartan finished chewing before answering. “I’m not an expert, but I think that if you give them the basic DNA, they’ll work with that. You’re the customer; they’ll provide what *you* want.”

Haldar looked at Toulis, “How soon can you get us a ship?”

Toulis stood up. “I’ll go outside to phone. Do you want a liner, or are cabins in a merchantman good enough?”

"So long as I don't have to ride outside wearing a spacesuit, I'm not too fussed," Haldar replied.

"Inside sounds good," Bartan agreed.

Toulis went outside. As he left, the waiter cleared away their plates. He returned in time to find the waiter setting three bowls on the table. Haldar was smiling broadly. "This you'll love, a real local delicacy, and they do it perfectly here."

Bartan prodded the contents of the dish with his spoon. "Dare I ask?"

"It's rice, cooked in milk, spiced with ginger, cinnamon, thickened with flour made from a local nut, and of course, with added sugar."

Bartan risked a spoonful. "I can cope with this." He ate a second spoonful with obvious relish. "So what's the catch?"

Haldar looked surprised. "No catch; Toulis, have we a ship?"

Toulis sat down and picked up his spoon. "Yes, a freighter, leaving tomorrow. I was told 17:00 local time, 'seeing as how I asked' but I get the impression they only dreamed up a time because I demanded one."

Bartan asked, "How long is the trip?"

"Three weeks. They've one stop-over on the way, but it's just to drop cargo; they've promised they won't be sitting round there waiting for more."

"How much is it going to cost?" Haldar asked.

Toulis kept his face expressionless. "I explained that I could pay in vouchers drawn on the Governor's Private Office. They offered me such a big discount for cash that I couldn't resist it, and Wayland Strang's organisation is paying. After all, they'd have expected to pay for me, and I'll book you two down as hired muscle."

"Seems fair enough," mused Bartan.

Haldar finished his desert and glanced at his phone. "Is that the time?" He stood up. "I've got to get back to Kaunas City. I've various things I'll have to clear from my desk before we leave. I'll have a taxi pick you up tomorrow morning, sometime after breakfast."

Toulis shook his head. "Such are the rewards of a life on the right side of the law. Starmancers and other undesirables spend their evenings carousing. Or so I've been reliably informed."

Haldar mimed mopping the tears from his eyes with a handkerchief and left, waving casually to the waiter as he did so. Bartan and Toulis settled down to finish the bottle of wine. The waiter made his way across, and for the first time that evening spoke to them. "Would the gentlemen like a liqueur to finish with?"

Toulis looked at Bartan. "I think I could cope with that."

Bartan nodded. "A most civilised way to finish the evening."

The waiter left, and returned with a tray. In front of each man he set a glass. Then he took a sheet of paper from the tray, which he handed to Toulis.

"Mr Hart?"

Toulis took the paper. "Yes?"

"The bill, sir; Mr Drom said you would be paying."

*****

Haldar met Bartan and Toulis at the Kaunas Space Port. The 'Serendipity' was a medium sized freighter, perhaps three times the size of the mercenary assault ship, but still capable of entering atmosphere. He watched as they unloaded their luggage from the rack at the back of the taxi.

"I see you've started dreaming again," Haldar said, nodding towards his two colleagues' bags. "Suddenly everyone's a musician, and I'm some uncultured barbarian from a backward planet where they've barely mastered fire, and are still not sure how to tax it."

Toulis hefted the starcaster in its carrying case. "Shh, don't spoil the good work. I've almost made an honest man of him."

Bartan glanced down at his own carrying case. "I've got to get ready for when news of this investigation reaches home and I'm forced to try a new career. Anyway, as Toulis pointed out, we'll have to make our own entertainment on this ship, and there is only so long you can spend writing up reports and crafting stylish and imaginative expenses claims."

They walked out across the scarred landing pad. The Serendipity was the centre of what little attention there was. Two people wearing exoskeletons were loading half-ton stackers off a flat trailer and into a cargo hold. As they approached, one of the exoskeletons stopped. A youngish woman raised herself up in the harness and shouted across.

"You lost?"

Haldar shouted back, "We're booked as passengers."

She gave him a wave, sank back into the harness and seemed to be talking into some sort of comm. From round the side of the ship ran a boy, aged perhaps twelve. He waved to the woman in the exoskeleton and ran across to the three men.

"You Mr Hart's party?"

Toulis stepped forward. "Yes, we are; three for Havadon Higher Orbital Facility."

The boy beamed enthusiastically at them. "Please come this way."

He turned and led them round to the other side of the Serendipity. There was a walkway up to a hatch above them. The boy gestured at the ship.

"Engine space at back, cargo forward, living quarters above and fuel in the gaps between. Welcome to Serendipity."

They followed him up the steps of the walkway and through the open airlock. Toulis ran his fingers over the hull. "Feel the surface; this ship is old."

Haldar asked "And when did you last see a new ship this far out in the Wisp?"

Bartan copied Toulis's action. "The surface feels rough."

Toulis said "Constant abrasion from dust and other debris in system. I'd guess three hundred years' worth, or thereabouts."

"Don't worry, Bartan," Haldar advised, "He's showing off, it's a loss adjusters' trick. A rascal who wants to sell a ship in a hurry will polish the area around the airlocks."

They stopped in a wide, open space. The boy indicated the room around him. "Main deck; they're just putting your quarters together."

Haldar looked round. The area was open, and a man and a woman were engaged in erecting panel walls. The woman stopped and looked at them. "Good, you're here. We've got the ablution tubes installed, just the panels to put up."

Haldar, Bartan and Toulis walked across to look at what was happening.

"I'm Shilla, captain of the Serendipity; this is Tongo, first mate, cook and my husband." She patted one of the panels. "They're a ply and Hexafoam sandwich; excellent noise insulation. Just slot the panels into the grooves set into the floor and ceiling to make a cubicle." She tapped one of the panels and grinned, "But they're not structural, so don't try to hang pictures on them."

Bartan looked round. "So what's the other side of the bulkheads?" "Forwards? That's the crew area, but it's also where you'll eat."

Bartan looked around the main deck. "There's a lot of empty space."

Shilla reached for the next panel. "Once we know how many passengers we have, we can fill the space with light cargo, the sort of stuff which is best shipped in-atmosphere and doesn't always come in stackers." She glanced round. "Mind you, we'll keep some space open if we can. It's always good to have somewhere for the kids to run around."

Tongo muttered something, and Shilla pushed firmly and helped him slide a panel into the slots. It clicked into place.

"Here is the final cubicle finished." Shilla opened a door in the panel and stepped back to let her passengers look in. "The ablutions tube is installed. It just locks in to the systems at the top and bottom. First time you use it be careful; occasionally someone gets hot and cold mixed up."

Toulis peered over Haldar's shoulder. "Ablution tube, bed, a chair, a small table."

Shilla nodded, "And if you look at the floor, it has a special panel we put down first. It's insulated, more pleasant on the feet than walking on the steel of the deck."

A hatch opened at the far end of the main deck and a stacker appeared. Shilla said, "Looks like they're loading this area. Provided everything is on the dock, we might be away in an hour after loading finishes."

She glanced at the three passengers. "Come through with me to the crew area, I'll show you the facilities. "

The facilities consisted of a dining area with a galley off to one side. The dining area had the sort of colour scheme only a four year old could love, and there were the prints of small paint-covered hands on the lower walls. "There's a drinks machine here; we stock it from the kitchen, so just help yourselves. Through that door is the crew quarters proper—imagine a lot of cubicles perhaps twice the size of yours." Shilla stopped. "Yes, twice the size. We've got half a dozen crew, plus family, so it's good to have some space on the main deck. We tend to use it as a lounge and children's play area." She gestured to another hatch. "Through that one and it's up to the bridge, down to engineering. The acceleration couches are in a bay at the back of the bridge."

She left them in the dining area with a hot drink each. Bartan looked at Toulis. "Children's play areas?"

Toulis nodded. "Yes, most freighters, unless they're running regular, short hauls, will have family on board."

"Isn't that just extra cost?" Haldar asked.

"Well, when you think about it, the employer is paying for the children anyway, and the general feeling is that any extra costs are cancelled out by quicker turnaround when you land on planet; no one wants leave to go and see family. The big liners don't do it, mind you;—screaming children playing all over the ship would probably shatter the illusion of opulence."

*****

Over the next couple of hours they got themselves settled in and reasonably comfortable. The main deck was starting to fill with half-ton stackers, as well as more general cargo. Eventually everything was properly secured, and it was about sunset by the time the Serendipity lifted off. A buzzer sounded throughout the ship, warning of acceleration, and Haldar, Bartan and Toulis strapped themselves into acceleration couches. Acceleration proved to be a steady two 'G', and Bartan asked why the couches were necessary. Tongo, strapped into a couch next to them, answered.

"We keep the acceleration low, especially with kids on board. The couches are mainly because of the risk of what Shilla calls 'rapid evasive manoeuvres.' You get all sorts of idiots flying in and out of spaceports." He looked gloomy. "Then you get local traffic over-flying them; we've had near collisions with everything from traffic cops to crop sprayers."

"So what is standard 'G' on this ship?" Toulis asked.

"One point one."

Bartan asked, "Is that because of having children on board, making sure they develop strong bones?"

Tongo turned to look at him, and Bartan could see a harrowed look in the man's eyes. "Never attempt to potty train a toddler at low 'G'." There was a long gap in the conversation, before Tongo muttered, "It took months to scrub the smell out of the atmosphere."

A second buzzer sounded and Tongo unclipped himself from the couch. "There'll be a meal ready in five minutes; I've just got to serve up." He made his way down to the galley area. The three passengers unstrapped themselves and followed him down. The rest of the crew started to drift into the dining area, and all sat around the one table. A gaggle of children clustered at the far end, away from the visitors. The young woman they had seen using the exoskeleton set out a bowl and spoon for everyone and said grace. Then Tongo placed a great dish of pasta in the middle of the table, and another dish of meat sauce. "We don't stand on ceremony, just serve yourselves. Among this crew it seems that showing even the slightest hint of appreciation is frowned upon, lest it encourage the cook to ask for a pay rise. "

He sat down and proceeded to put a ladle full of pasta into his dish, pouring another ladle of meat sauce over it. He passed the pasta ladle to Haldar on his right. "Now to introduce the company; you'll be with us for at least three weeks, so you might as well get to know us. Me, you know. Shilla, as captain, is still on the bridge; I'll take her meal up to her. This young lady is Patti, cargo loader and paramedic, the man next to her is her husband Lallan, professional gambler and relief cook."

Toulis interrupted, "Professional gambler?"

Lallan gave a dour smile. "I'm not allowed to play on shipboard, and certainly not with passengers. I'm not really a crew member, but I can cook and help to dispel the air of gloom that emanates from the galley when Tongo is cooking. "

Tongo continued. "The couple next to him are Fingle, our engineer, and his wife, Zenobia, who drives the second exoskeleton."

"I'm not really crew either," Zenobia interrupted, "but I help out with loading and unloading. I'm also a nurse and trained in child care."

Tongo sailed briskly on, "And we have Harper; she's our second engineer," he said, picking out a motherly woman in her forties. "And sitting next to her is her husband Wingo, who is an ex-Navy weapons-tech, and handles the light laser turret, plus all our electrics and navigational systems. But mainly he makes models of ships in the workshop and sells them around the ports when we dock."

Tongo lapsed into silence as he ate his own meal. There was a low hum of conversation, which was limited to matters of import such as 'pass the salt please' and 'any sauce left?'

Eventually people finished, and the bowls were passed down to the end of the table. Then a young girl disappeared into the galley and came back carrying a cake. She placed it in front of Tongo. "This is the dessert, Tongo," she said, with intense earnestness.

Tongo contemplated the cake. "Would you like to cut a slice, young lady? Then I can try it; see if it's fit for guests."

She nodded, realised there was no knife and bolted for the galley. She came back with the knife and, with immense care, cut a slice of cake and manoeuvred it onto a plate. The plate she passed to Tongo, who cautiously picked up the piece of cake and studied it. He was holding it carefully; it had been cut remarkably thin. He bit off a piece and chewed it meditatively. Without comment he ate the rest. There was silence round the table. The children especially were watching Tongo like hawks.

Eventually, the masticated cake swallowed, Tongo spoke.

"Well, it's very good, but … ." With the 'but' the girl started to look very serious.

After soaking the pause for its drama, Tongo continued. "It tastes of knife."

The girl looked perplexed and studied the knife blade carefully. Zenobia reached across the table and tapped the girl on the arm.

"What the great loon means is that next time, cut him a thick piece, not one so thin he could read a newspaper through." She smiled at the girl to encourage her. "Now cut the cake into sensible pieces and pass it round.

*****

Haldar awoke suddenly, aware he could hear something, but not sure what it was. He listened and there, on the edge of hearing, was music. He couldn't place where it was coming from, but then there was a woman's voice, singing. He glanced at his watch. He'd slept in and probably missed breakfast. He sat up on the bed and listened to the singing. It was louder now, more confident. At this point, he realised that for the first time in his life, he could legitimately use the word 'raunchy'. It wasn't a word much used in the sort of reports he had to write. Not only that, but back when he was a naval officer, they'd habitually used shorter words to describe the same sort of effect. As he dressed, the singing continued, and when he opened the door of his cubicle the full volume of the music hit him. He glanced out into the main deck and looked for the source. Sitting on packing crates, playing their starcasters, were Bartan and Toulis, while standing in front of them Patti was singing.

When they saw him, the musicians stopped. Bartan asked, "What did you think of it?"

Haldar made a gesture of resignation. "I suppose I could say that Hexafoam isn't as good a sound insulator as I thought. But what I heard was alright. I'm off to see if there's any breakfast."

Patti said, "I've got us a professional booking."

Haldar looked surprised. "Where?"

"The Havadon Higher Orbital." She perhaps sensed his scepticism, then added, "Alright, I've not actually got the booking yet, but the bars on the middle levels will take pretty well anyone; I've sung there before, and these two are as good as most backing musicians."

"I've seen it all now," Haldar sighed. "I hope at least these two will remember their old friends when they're rich and famous." He turned towards the dining area. "But if you can spare them, it'd be nice to have a chat about what we're going to do when we get to the Higher Orbital. Free improvisation might be fashionable in musical circles, but I'm unfashionable enough to think we ought to plan a little."

The other two joined him after he'd eaten, and Patti had gone back on shift. They adjourned to Haldar's cubicle, Bartan and Toulis fetching their own chairs.

Haldar asked the question he hoped the others had been thinking about. "Will Grorin-Tech talk to us?"

Toulis asked "Are we officials, customers or what?"

"I'm assuming Grorin-Tech may have heard about the destruction of their facility on Tsarina, but I don't think they will know the details of what has happened, and I had thought of approaching them as part of the official investigation. We do have the samples which they might be interested in."

Toulis looked pensive. "I didn't really want to have to tell you gentlemen, but I have this." He reached into an inside pocket and pulled out his wallet. From it he produced a plastic strip about the length and breadth of his little finger.

Haldar asked, "What is it?"

"A Grorin-Tech sample key; it's for the seriously wealthy only. If you have a medical emergency, they plug this key into their system and it gives them a complete breakdown of your genetics. Using it, they can then grow any bit you need more quickly than otherwise. Also, your nearest Grorin-Tech facility will have a selection of your organs, skin, blood and suchlike, pre-generated and just waiting for you."

He returned the plastic strip to his wallet and put it back in his pocket. "If Grorin-Tech have a genetic breakdown of your samples on file, they can compare them with this key, and see if there any similarities."

There was silence, and then Haldar asked, "Why didn't you tell us earlier? I hate to say it, but I get nervous when I'm drip-fed information."

Toulis smiled weakly. "Actually, I rather like you gentlemen. Think about it. Let us assume that someone has been running a scheme to humiliate Mr Strang. When he finds out about it, Mr Strang might just want to eliminate anyone he doesn't trust who knows about the scheme. Hell, I don't even know if he trusts me enough to let me live."

There was further silence. Bartan pushed his chair back. "Have we done enough planning?"

Haldar muttered "Yeah, sure," then he looked at Bartan. "I think we've got a plan. Are you happy with it?"

Bartan grinned at him. "Happy enough; anyway if it's alright with you, I'm off to practice the starcaster. Patti is a pretty exacting boss. Also, I guess it'll be easier to make a living on the run from a Starmancer as a jobbing musician than as a police officer."

Chapter 5

The Havadon Higher Orbital Facility hung in space like some obscene spider with a huge bloated body and atrophied spindly limbs. Gantries and access tubes dangled passively from what convention dictated was 'the bottom' and slab-sided sewage scows, bulk water transports and liquid air tankers clustered down there. On the Facility's hull, clinging like fleas on a dog, were the ships on the external docking bays. Then there were the gaping maws of the internal bays, where the pampered queens of space, the liners, would berth.

When seen from a closer vantage point, the hull itself looked as if it had been attacked by a horde of barely literate vandals armed with spray paint in industrial quantities. In letters often many feet high were instructions for space lines (long lapsed into the final oblivion of bankruptcy) to use various bays. Other instructions were merely to maintenance gangs, 'thin plate/ replace' or 'renew patches' with arrows which had presumably pointed to the site to be tackled. Messages had been painted over messages; whole words disappeared when plates were replaced, crude doodles appeared where bored repairmen had imaginatively reinterpreted existing marks.

Haldar estimated that the Facility was perhaps ten miles in diameter, with internal docking bays large enough to take the Taurus, never mind the Serendipity. He had watched it grow large on the screen as they strapped themselves into the acceleration couches. But now the screen showed the Serendipity, as Shilla had patched through a view from the cameras on the Facility. Shilla was manoeuvring the Serendipity onto one of the external docking bays, using a mixture of automatics and gentle manual override.

Haldar watched with some admiration as the Serendipity moved slowly sideways and down, so that she landed on a metal shelf sticking out at right-angles to the surface. There was a slight jolt as the magnetic clamps on the landing gear were energised and the ship dropped the last few inches and then locked in place. Now Haldar could see on the screen that the metal shelf was being retracted into the Facility, and the access port was being lined up with the ship's main loading bay. The ship halted and they could hear the clang as the access port tube contacted the side of the ship. The view on the screen switched to the inside of the tube. Vac-suited technicians were clamping the tube to the ship and spraying foam sealant along the join to prevent air leaking out into space. Finally, one of the technicians stopped, facing the camera, glanced at a monitor, gave a thumbs-up sign and opened the front of his helmet.

Shilla shouted from the bridge, 'We have atmosphere in the tube; who's ready to go ashore?"

Haldar glanced at Toulis and Bartan. "Are you two artistes ready to disembark?"

Toulis answered for both of them. "Yes, Patti and Lallan are taking the starcasters with them when Patti's finished unloading and loading. They'll let us know where to meet her later."

Haldar got up from the couch and picked up the small, refrigerated bag from the floor at his feet. "Let's go and get it over with, then."

The three men made their way to the Main Deck. Zenobia opened a hatch and lowered the walkway. Below them, Patti had already got the main hatch open and her exoskeleton out. She was starting to pick up the stackers and put them in a pile in the tube.

"I'd better get moving as well," Zenobia said as she led them down the walkway. "Just go along the tube, through the first bulkhead into the stacking chamber. Shut the door and then open the next door, it'll get you onto the main freight distribution route. When you're out onto the route, shut the door behind you and then the first bulk head door will open again. The stacking chamber acts as an airlock. We'll offload into there, and then load from there into a freight hauler. They do it that way to make sure some clown with an exoskeleton doesn't vent half the atmosphere out to vacuum because he can't tell his left from his right and walks through the wall of the tube."

"Does that often happen?" Haldar asked, surprised.

"More often than you'd believe," Zenobia answered. "You'd be amazed who gets to play with exoskeletons on some ships."

Haldar, Bartan and Toulis made their way along the tube. Its walls were of some sort of metal concertina which showed occasionally through gaps in the airtight fabric fastened to it. The edges of the gaps were thick with spray-on sealant. On the wall were three lights. The green light was flashing, the amber glowed slightly, and the red remained dark,

Toulis took a deep breath. "Green light flashing, air pressure in here is fair, but not what I'd call good."

"Probably best if we don't hang around then," Bartan said as he licked a finger and held it up to see if he could detect air movement. "This area is somewhat rougher than the liner dock. At least the liner dock is properly air-sealed."

He led off down towards the bulkhead door. The other two followed him. Toulis said as an aside "I know the liner dock; I've been there when travelling for work; not only is it internal, with a bulkhead door that shuts to seal it from space, it has an inner tube that passengers walk down, which hides the outer tube. When the outer tubes from the liner dock start to look worn, they're replaced with new ones, and the old ones are put into store to use as replacements for the lower freight decks."

At the bulkhead door, Toulis stopped to read the painted slogan, 'The Bar Rolando for the best in boys, girls and beer.' Haldar read it over his shoulder. "That where Patti has got you playing?"

Toulis shrugged. Bartan tapped the buttons on the keypad and they could hear the air hiss past them as the pressure equalised. The door opened and they stepped quickly inside the large chamber and closed the door behind them. At the next door they equalised the pressure again, opened the door and stepped into the freight distribution route. Toulis sniffed appreciatively. "Ah, the smell of a space station; an interesting mix of old grease, overloaded electrical components and unwashed humanity." He looked across to Bartan.

"You wouldn't believe how much trouble they take to try and keep this aroma out of the upper levels."

"Do they manage?" Haldar asked.

"Not really," Toulis replied, "it's just that by the time you find your way about, your nose is acclimatised." He looked round. "I'd say along the freight route and then down one of the corridors off."

They hugged the interior wall, and were occasionally passed by freight haulers, long low vehicles with a driver sitting at one end, steering. The corridor off was marked by an arrow painted on the floor, pointing to a small door. The door itself wasn't an airlock, but was self-sealing. Painted on it with some sort of white marker was the message 'Stiggy, we'll be at Effens'. It opened away from them into the corridor, and when Bartan, the last man through, let go of it, it slammed shut. After walking along perhaps forty yards of graffiti-decorated corridor, they came to a meeting of several corridors and a twin lift shaft. Lift plates, seemingly featureless ceramic discs not quite the diameter of the shaft, rose constantly out of one shaft and descended constantly down the other. The circuitry embedded within the ceramic functioned both as a weak gravitic motor and as a guidance mechanism which held them in place relative to each other and to the walls.

Bartan looked at Toulis. "Up, I assume?"

"Yes, quite a way; from memory, we want Upper Deck Three."

Toulis stepped onto a plate as it passed, and Bartan and Haldar scrambled to join him. The plate swayed slightly and then righted itself and continued on its stately way up.

They were on the lift for about twenty minutes, watching an endless succession of corridors go past. Some would be decorated with the names of spaceships, some with the names of bars or other businesses found on that level. The higher they got, the more respectable the communication. Occasionally, they would see people waiting for a plate. Haldar assumed that locally it was considered impolite to get onto a plate that was already occupied. In the lower levels, it tended to be techs and ships crews travelling. One crew all wore one-piece coveralls in the same colour. Toulis identified them as crew from 'The Cloud', a ship with a postal contract, so could afford to dock in an internal bay. The crew regarded themselves as a cut above the rest, though that opinion was not widely shared.

At one point, they broke out into a large open area, with vegetation and even a fountain in the distance, before they passed and there was nothing but corridors again. Now the people boarding or leaving plates tended to be dressed in brightly coloured sarongs. Haldar noticed a family group, their sarongs obviously cut from the same roll of cloth. As they got higher the people they saw were more cosmopolitan, businessmen and merchant traders from around the cluster.

Each corridor had a numeral painted on it. Haldar gestured toward one sign as they passed, "Upper Deck Six".

"Yes, they number from the top. Better get ready to step off now."

They moved to the edge of the plate; Haldar could feel it sag slightly before the automatics balanced things up. Two more corridors passed before Haldar saw the sign, Upper Deck Three.

"This is our level, everyone off," Toulis declared. The three of them stepped off and looked around. The corridor was comparatively short, perhaps ten yards long, and then there was a ninety-degree bend. They walked down the corridor, white painted and lit by concealed lighting. Behind them, lift plates continued to pass up and down. Once round the corner, the corridor opened abruptly into an open space. Haldar looked around. There was a gap between the ceiling forty feet above his head, and a suspended ceiling six feet below it. Through the gap he could see a mass of pipes, tubes, cable ducts and other services. The suspended ceiling itself was a holographic projection of the sky on a world Haldar didn't recognise. Birds flew, clouds blew slowly over, and there was even flitter traffic. In front of him was a diamond-shaped open area, and around it clustered various shop fronts. At a quick guess, there could be anywhere up to a hundred fronts visible in this diamond alone. Scattered about the centre of the diamond were small bars and cafes with seats arrayed around them.

Toulis said "The fronts are just fronts; some establishments are all on this level, and others have space booked on the level above and the level below. The idea is that they can all have their reception here, and you can find anyone. There are another three of these diamonds on this floor. They make up the permanent trade fair."

"Looks like every front is taken," Haldar said as they walked across the diamond.

"They always are. If they cannot get a tenant for one, there is a lottery down on Havadon, and a small firm from Havadon gets the place for three years, rent free. It keeps the place looking full and busy, and also keeps rents sensible."

At the far side of the diamond, Bartan stopped and with a flourish pointed to a particularly impressive shop front. "Behold the door to the Grorin-Tech centre. Gentlemen, we have arrived."

*****

Haldar studied the shop front with interest. The door was merely a curtain of shimmering beads, which somehow served to stop all sound passing. Next to the door was a display area. Some shops had made do with windows, and behind the glass you could see machine tools, foodstuffs, working models of engineering projects, mannequins clothed in exquisite fabrics. Some, mainly accountants, lawyers or brokers would often make do with a view into the busy office on the other side of the window. Their staff were frantically busy using communications devices, or consulting what appeared to be legal documents.

Grorin-Tech, on the other hand, had a holo-display instead of a window. As he watched, Haldar saw laughing, healthy children, beautiful women in garments considered elegant in a score of the more sophisticated planetary systems and burly workers good naturedly labouring in fields, factories or mines.

"It's a continuous loop," Bartan said. "The operating theatre footage is interesting, but probably not worth waiting for." He moved towards the curtain of shimmering beads. "Should we go in?"

On the other side of the curtain was a small office. There was a stairway which led both up and down, but access to the stair was controlled by a desk, manned by a disarmingly pretty girl who watched them enter.

"Greetings, gentlemen; how may Grorin-Tech be of assistance?"

The other two hung back, leaving Haldar in the lead. "I represent the Government of Tsarina, and I'd like to discuss a Grorin-Tech facility on Tsarina."

The girl pursed her lips. "I think this may be a matter for Technician Janson." She pressed a series of buttons on her desk and studied something visible only to her. "Yes, our doorman is coming to guide you to Technician Janson's office."

A tall male figure appeared in the stairwell behind her, held his hand, palm outwards in front of him, and a transparent screen slid to one side. He stepped into the office. "Gentlemen, follow me please."

Silently he led them down the stairs, the screen closing behind them. On the next level down he led them through a brightly lit meeting area and stopped.

"I am to take you to see Technician Janson. He is the senior customer-facing executive in Wilbur's Wisp."

"Technician?" Haldar asked, "that's an unusual title for an executive."

"All personnel who have achieved the second initiation are addressed as Technician, sir. For us, that is more important than temporary rank within the organisation."

Their guide knocked on the third door they came to. It opened and he gestured for them to enter. "Technician Janson's office, sirs."

The man sitting behind the desk came as something of a surprise. He wore a full face helmet, the visor mirrored so that the face was invisible. Haldar knew that some pilots favoured them; to see what was happening in the real world in front of them, they would patch across to a camera. When he spoke, Janson's voice was slightly distorted, as if he was using a throat mike and speaker.

"Gentlemen, how may Grorin-Tech be of assistance?"

Haldar stepped forward and presented his ID document. "I am Haldar Drom of the Tsarina Governors Investigation Office. I'm making inquiries about a Grorin-Tech facility which was situated on Tsarina." He placed a second document on the desk. "This is my warrant, extending my authority and empowering me to deal with the matter under the Wilbur's Wisp co-responsibility agreement."

Janson inspected the documents, but his manner remained formal. After a while, Haldar suspected that Janson would always remain formal. "I have here all our files about the Tsarina facility. I would note that it does not appear to have violated any laws or regulations of Tsarina."

"Only because our laws and regulations were drawn up by someone who wanted the job finished in time for an early lunch,' Haldar thought, but he kept that to himself. Instead he asked, "It is not our belief that Grorin-Tech acted illegally."

Janson cut across him. "You refer to the facility in the past tense?"

Haldar managed to keep his face straight. There were at least some things they didn't know. "Yes, it was destroyed by a major explosion, and that is part of the reason for our investigation."

Janson was silent for a while; Haldar suspected he was updating files and sending out the information. Then Janson asked, "How did this come about?"

"We're not entirely sure. There was unauthorised activity in the area, and we currently believe it may have been a self-destruct mechanism."

"The Tsarina facility was not fitted with a self-destruct mechanism." Janson's reply was definite. Haldar would not have been surprised if the Technician had the plans displayed on his head-up display as they talked.

"In which case, it may have been fitted later."

"That would be most irregular."

“It is the irregularities of the case that interest us. We have samples of various pre-fertilised genotypes that were installed.”

“May I see them?”

Haldar handed the man the refrigerated sample bag. The tech opened the bag and passed a hand scanner over the individual packets. “These are all genotypes licensed to the facility.”

Haldar produced the empty carton marked Genotype 1a/ Croton.

Janson held the scanner to the label. “This is not one of ours; it is obviously something made locally.” His voice sounded disdainful. “Occasionally we discover that our business partners do venture into the unlicensed market. It is not in breach of contract, but we do warn against it.”

“Do you know who is named on the licence?” Haldar asked.

“Yes, but the licence was held by a holding company, the shareholders of which were also holding companies.”

There was a pause as Haldar thought. Then he asked, “Would Liadan Consolidated Securities be one of those companies?”

There was a brief silence from Janson, during which Haldar assumed that the tech was wondering how much to disclose. “Obviously, I cannot breach client confidentiality, but that company does hold some of the shares directly.”

Toulis moved closer to Haldar and muttered “LCS? They’re a big customer of mine.”

Haldar turned and winked at him, “Doran has family connections with them. I’d check their claims record, if I were you.” He turned back to Janson. “Do you have the DNA and associated data for those sample genotypes?”

“Yes, they are all on file here, except for Genotype 1a/ Croton, for which we have no data.”

“If my friend here gives you a Grorin-Tech sample key, could you read it and say whether there are similarities between it and the samples?”

Again the pause, then Janson came to a decision. “If you have secondary authorisation to go with the sample key, the answer is yes.”

Toulis reached into his jacket and produced both the sample key and a second plastic strip, of similar size, which he handed to Janson. Janson slid both into a reader built into the desk. He withdrew them and handed them back to Toulis. “Yes, I am authorised to tell you. The match between the samples and key is excellent. I am forced to assume that the person whose key you have given me is the person who supplied the initial genetic material.”

Toulis laid a hand on Haldar’s shoulder to forestall his next question and asked “Does it show on your files how and when the initial genetic material entered your system?”

"It appears that the key-holder gave permission just over six standard years ago, perhaps a year before the genotypes were created."

Toulis said quickly, "*Appears?*"

"The nature of the permission is not documented." Janson's voice sounded distracted. "Ah, here it is; a note that it was authorisation was via courier, who carried on them appropriate authorisation."

Haldar casually asked "Are you allowed to tell us what genotypes were made, just so we know what the samples are?"

Janson replied without pause. "You have the samples; you can work it out for yourself within a few months, and hence, confidentiality isn't breached by telling you. There was a range of genotypes created. Some were standard; for some reason, field workers are popular. We assume that people buy many genotypes with the intention that the out-crossing will produce hybrid vigour while keeping the docility. There were also maintenance techs—"

Here Haldar interrupted, "are they the three-foot-tall idiot savants?"

"The preferred term is 'appropriately sized, with appropriate intelligence,'" Janson answered smoothly, "but yes, they're the ones. We also have here a short run of thin atmosphere types. They're unusual; we probably had an order in when we were working on the sample, and produced a few because patrons obviously want a wide variety of genotypes in their new population."

Haldar asked "So all these would be available in both male and female then?"

"Yes. Obviously, you'd need a population which bred true, but there are only certain traits that you would lock in; other traits would be allowed to drift to try and counter the effect of having too small a gene pool."

"You said they were the standard ones; were there any non-standard ones?"

Janson's voice remained emotionless. "Yes, several different types. There was a female escort variant; these are widely popular on a huge variety of worlds. There was also a male variant."

"A male escort?" Haldar asked.

"Yes, more specialist, tailored to suit the more specialist and discerning male and female clientele. We tend to enhance the musculature, as well as make them naturally depilated." Janson seemed to be contemplating something. "There is one here I must confess that I never noticed. A naturally coprophagous modification, created with the idea being that they would be maintenance techs for a sewage system." Janson seemed to be musing aloud. "An interesting concept, bold even; but I cannot understand why there was an insistence on a strong hereditability of facial features."

"Oh, I can," said Toulis quietly.

Janson seemed to be lost in thought, so Haldar asked "is that it?"

"I think that is all I can tell you; given the samples you have fetched me."

"Can you give me an idea of how many may have been born?"

Janson was briefly silent. "No, that isn't data we collect. But I can tell you that over seven thousand units were delivered, and the facility was live for some years. So assuming standard work rates, perhaps four thousand are now implanted or have experienced parturition."

"And all these produce self-replicating populations?"

"No, both male and female escorts are naturally infertile. Clients seem to prefer it."

Toulis said, in a small voice, "I think I need a drink. Does coprophagous mean what I think it means?"

"Dung eating," Bartan answered. "We've a fine selection of coprophagous insects on New Charity." As Toulis stared at him he added, defensively, "We're an agricultural world, everyone knows this kind of stuff."

Haldar turned away from his two colleagues and looked back to Janson. "My superiors will probably be in touch with Grorin-Tech. Until then, I am sure you can understand that we would be grateful if you didn't mention this discussion with anyone outside your organisation."

"And especially with our client?" Janson asked.

"I would not like it to prejudice our investigation."

Janson's voice remained impassive. "I doubt the topic will arise in discussion, and if not raised, we will not raise it." Janson pressed a button. "Our doorman will escort you out."

*****

Toulis slumped in a chair at the nearest bar. "He is going to go berserk," he intoned, to on one in particular. Bartan thrust a drink into his hand. Toulis looked at the drink without it appearing to register. "He'll kill us all, and probably everyone else, as well."

Bartan guided Toulis' hand to his mouth. "Come on, drink up. It might not be that bad."

"Not that bad? I've got to waltz into his office and say 'excuse me, Sir, but six years ago someone very senior in your organisation handed your DNA over to Grorin-Tech and now you're the proud father of a race of shit eating, barely sentient, sewer maintenance techs." He drank off his drink in one. "Oh yes, and every tart and catamite in fifty systems is going to look like you as well." Toulis drained his glass. "And there is nothing he can do about it. His *children* are out there, on scores of worlds."

Bartan asked "Is he even on this orbital?"

"I haven't a clue. Remember, people don't meet him anymore. There are pictures about of what he used to look like, but he needn't look like that anymore." Toulis lowered his voice. "He could be that man sitting three tables away, flicking through a magazine."

"Well, you don't actually have to tell him. You can tell that 'friend' of his who briefed you," Haldar said, thoughtfully.

"For all I know, that might have been him."

Haldar ignored the interruption. "That way, someone else has to tell Wayland Strang, and by the time your reticent employer becomes coherent again, we'll be back on the Serendipity and heading for home."

Toulis sat and stared into space as if doing some arcane arithmetic in his head.

"Right," he said, standing up. "We find Patti; we play this venue for her. We might just be three middle-aged men trying not to grow up, but we need not let her down. Then she makes damned sure the ship is ready to leave. Bartan gets the first boat he can for New Charity."

"Not an issue; there are shuttles down to Havadon every hour, and at least one grain barge returns home to New Charity every day," Bartan said.

As if he hadn't heard him, Toulis continued, "Haldar gets onto the Serendipity with Patti, and I tell 'the friend'. I get back to the Serendipity, and the ship leaves. If I don't get back within the hour, I think you might be best to just leave anyway."

Haldar looked at Bartan and shrugged, "Well, it's a plan."

"I cannot think of a better one," Bartan said, a note of sadness in his voice. "I think we have to go with it."

*****

As Haldar finished his drink and Toulis stared into space, Bartan walked off to one side and contacted Patti by comm. He re-joined the others, "We have to meet her on Lower Deck Three."

Toulis came out of his reverie. "She's got us playing a classy joint. The crowd on Lower Deck Three probably won't attempt to eat you."

Haldar stood up. "If they've evolved to that level of sophistication, we'd better not keep your fans waiting"

They made their way back to the lift and stepped on a passing plate. Haldar thought Toulis was recovering a little, and by the time they arrived at Lower Deck Three he even had something of a swagger in his step. Patti and Lallan met them, Lallan carrying the two starcasters and Patti wearing a long coat which virtually touched the ground as she walked.

"Successful day?"

Haldar nodded. "Well, we've discovered what the facility in the Border Kingdoms was producing, and we suspect we know why they were doing it. We don't know who destroyed it, but we've found out a lot of what we came to find out. So after you good people have gone through your act, we'd better be ready to leave really quickly."

"You've not got a lot of confidence in their musical ability have you?" Lallan said dryly.

Haldar shook his head. "They could be brilliant, but trust me, in a couple of hours, it would be better if the Serendipity was on her way."

Patti glanced at him. "You're serious aren't you? What have you three been up to?"

Bartan said gently "Don't ask, you really don't want to know. Trust me in that. How soon can your ship leave?"

"Cargo shipment is done before we go off duty. It is possible that Shilla or Wingo might find some more, but that would be extra. So I suppose Shilla could take us out as soon as she had port clearance, if she needed to, and with an external berth, that's not going to take more than the time it takes to unhook the tube and traffic control gives us a course to steer away from the Orbital."

Haldar smiled at her. "Good. If you can get hold of Shilla on the comm and let her know, we'll be able to enjoy ourselves for an hour or so."

Patti reached for her comm while Lallan led the three men through an open door wide enough to drive a freight hauler through.

Inside, the space was gloomy compared to the concourse, and was made even more gloomy by having an apparently random selection of booths scattered along the walls. A bar stood towards one end, with a raised area near it. The raised area was brightly lit.

"That," Lallan said gesturing toward the light, "is what passes as a stage."

As they walked through, Haldar noticed that about half the booths had drinkers sitting in them and there were a few more at the bar.

"Don't worry, it'll fill up later when people know there's a show." Patti sounded confident.

A short man, running to fat, squeezed out from behind the bar and came to join them. "Patti, good to see you, we've got everything ready. You play the first set and then perhaps a few encores?"

Lallan said "That will suit us, Zeewan. Next time, you'll want them as the main attraction, not just the warm-up band."

Zeewan raised both hands in a gesture of surrender. "All right, I realise the opening slot isn't the best, but you have to work your way up in this trade."

Patti made a dismissive gesture, a wave with her left hand. "If I'm good enough, you'll want me back; if I'm not, then you're right to put me on first. But …" and here she stepped closer to him, "it would be a nice gesture to pay the money now."

She held out her hand. Zeewan pulled a bundle of notes out of his pocket and counted six into her hand. Patti said nothing, but just kept her hand open. Zeewan sighed and counted out another two. He glanced up at Patti's face, then sighed again and counted out another two. "For that money, you *should* be the main act."

Patti smiled sweetly at him. "For that money, Lallan doesn't gamble here, and I forget about all the little indiscretions of your youth."

"You're as hard a woman as your mother was, Patti." Zeewan sighed a third time. "But there are so few of the old crowd left." He walked back to the bar, seemingly shrunken.

Lallan looked around the stage area. "Well, they've got the plugs and pick-ups ready. It'll take perhaps five minutes and then you can tune up and start."

Haldar moved across to Toulis and Bartan. "There is a man sitting in the third booth past the bar. On his own, well dressed."

Bartan nodded, "I see him."

"I know him, Bilhar Tilwash. He's a senior member of the Tsarina diplomatic service. Very close to Doran Stilan. What's he doing here?"

Lallan leaned across from where he was checking a socket. "Zeewan runs a good bar, safe, straight. Men can do business here."

"He might know me," Haldar said. "I think I better find myself somewhere inconspicuous."

Patti looked round, and then waved to a girl leaning against the bar. The girl came across. "Haldar, I want you to meet my friend, Jeana. She's second engineer on the Tyro. Jeana, this is Haldar, a friend of mine who doesn't want people to notice him. How about you take him into the second booth past the bar, let him buy you a drink and lie to you about how beautiful you are?"

Jeana combed her hair hastily with stained fingers. "Well, it's the best offer I've had this evening." She took Haldar's arm and led him across to the booth. Patti turned to Bartan and Toulis. "Well, that's him hidden, how about we start tuning up?"

*****

When Toulis slowly played the opening chords of their first number, Patti signalled to Lallan, who dimmed the lights around them, leaving one picking out Patti. She shrugged off her coat and stood there in a long silver dress that clung to her figure. Toulis played a few swift chords and ripples of colour and transparency ran across the dress.

There were a few whistles from the darkness, and Patti swirled the dress a little before launching into the song. Haldar watched for a few moments, and decided that things seemed to be going well enough. He got out a comm.

Jeana watched him in disapproving silence. "My Mam always told me it was bad manners to play with one of them when you were with company."

Haldar tapped the comm with a fore finger. "Just let me change the settings, then I'll clamp it to the wall. Could you just stand up with your back to the bar, as if you were talking to me? Then I can get it set up."

Somewhat mystified, Jeana did as she was asked. Hurriedly, Haldar clamped the comm to the wall and tweaked the settings delicately.

"He's got a shield up to prevent being overheard, but I think I can beat it." Haldar shifted the settings a little more and screwed something that looked like a pen into the back of the comm. He listened to an earpiece. "I think that's it. But he's still on his own. I won't really know until he has company." Haldar glanced up at Jeana, "Oh, and you can sit down now."

*****

Toulis played. His was the lesser part. Bartan carried the tune and Patti covered up their faults. As he played, he watched. He wasn't sure what he was watching for, but he was sure Wayland Strang, or at least his senior people, would know he was on the Orbital. So far, they hadn't done anything about it. They might not, but they might put someone to watch him, and he wanted to know who the watchers were. So far he'd seen no one he knew. Then, perhaps two thirds of the way through their set, someone came in he did recognise; Little Kaidar, captain of the Falling Angel. Toulis tried to keep his head down and moved slightly to put Patti between Kaidar and himself. To his relief and surprise, Kaidar bought a drink and went and sat in the same booth as Bilhar Tilwash.

The set continued, and when they finished there was applause, some of it sincere. Patti whispered "Gone." And Toulis launched into the chords of their encore piece. Bartan joined him and then Patti started singing. No subtle ballad, this was a bar girl's declaration of war on an uncaring universe. Even as he played, Toulis felt that it was the best thing they'd done. Eventually, as the final strident chords died away, the applause started, and this time it was genuine. Even the bar staff were applauding. Lallan dimmed the main light and quietly the three performers moved away from the stage and stood round the back of the bar. There they passed the next act moving out to the stage.

The lead singer put a hand on Patti's arm. "You sang it, girl, you sang it." She smiled at him and squeezed his hand. The others moved on and Patti turned to Bartan and Toulis. "Thanks, you two. You were good." Toulis kissed her.

"It was fun. Now I've got to go, so make sure you get yourselves away to the ship in time." He handed his starcaster to Lallan. "Could you look after this for me? It probably won't help my image where I'm going." He made his way between the drinkers, who were now sitting or standing in the middle of the floor, watching the next band set up.

"Always have to be the centre of attention, don't you?" The voice was male, and was larded with contempt.

Patti tensed. Bartan noted she placed her left hand on Lallan's chest to stop him moving forward. Then she stepped forward, like a dangerous animal preparing to pounce. "Still here are you, Bern?" She spat the words. "You've been sitting at this bar so long you've worn grooves in it with your elbows."

Bern expectorated on the floor by her feet. "You always did have a big mouth."

Patti's left foot whipped out, hooked round the leg of the stool Bern was sitting on and pulled. Bern crashed heavily to the floor, flat on his back.

"Bern, you're so full of shit, your eyes are brown."

"Why you mad bitch, I'll..."

At this point, Bartan's foot rested firmly on Bern's right hand. Bartan bent down and casually pulled a knife from the cross sheath Bern worn above his belt buckle. He glanced at the knife. "Ceramic; interesting, but unwise." He tossed the knife behind the bar, out of the way. "Were you thinking of saying anything else?" Bartan asked conversationally. He applied a little more pressure to Bern's right hand.

"No."

"That didn't sound convincing," Bartan said quietly. "Are you sure?"

Zeewan appeared at Bartan's elbow, two burly men next to him.

"You know the rules, Bern," Zeewan said, his voice quiet. "I don't like people picking fights in my bar. There are two of my boys here want a word with you, perhaps teach you a few manners outside."

Bern looked up and paled. Bartan spoke quietly into Zeewan's ear. "Let's not have any violence. I'm going down to the surface. Your two friends can escort Bern to the shuttle with me, and I'll make sure he gets down to the ground. He'll probably not have the fare back, so he can cool his heels down there and be someone else's problem."

Zeewan showed his teeth and reached down into Bern's shirt and pulled out a wallet. He flicked through it. "He might just have enough for a ticket down."

He looked down at Bern. "Bon Voyage."

The two burly men hauled Bern roughly to his feet and led him away. Bartan turned to face Patti. "I've got to go now. I'll see him off the Orbital, if nothing else."

Patti kissed him. "Thanks, it was good working with you."

Bartan turned to go, and then turned back. "Just out of interest, who was he?"

"Bern? My ex-husband."

*****

To any casual observer, Haldar was just another man cuddled up close to a pretty girl in a bar. He noticed Toulis leave, he saw Bartan leave with Patti and Lallan following shortly after. But his head was resting on the comm clamped to the booth wall. Eventually, he had given up fiddling with it and had come to the conclusion that with the technology he had to hand there was a limit to how reliably he could breach Tilwash's shield. He was forced to concentrate and see what he could piece together from the scraps that he did manage to glean.

He could tell when Tilwash was joined by someone. A conversation of growls and whistles started, punctuated by the occasional string of coherent words. Wayland Strang was mentioned, often in a derogatory fashion. Haldar got the feeling that Tilwash was offering someone an opportunity, certainly wealth, and perhaps even authority came into it. Whoever he was talking to seemed cautious, perhaps even dismissive, at least initially. Yet as the conversation continued, Haldar had the feeling that the person had been won over. All this took a considerable amount of time, but there was a growing sense of good fellowship, and as the two men parted, the one who wasn't Tilwash said 'men have got tired of just drawing their wage, they want to be Starmancers again.' Tilwash just laughed and said something about "they'll enjoy their visit to Tsarina."

The booth next to him went quiet, and after a couple of minutes he got Jeana to visit the ladies. When she arrived back, she reported the booth next to them was unoccupied. Haldar unclipped his comm and slipped it in his pocket. He looked out of the booth. Tilwash was just visible, walking out of the door. Making his excuses, Haldar followed him, walking briskly to the exit and looking out across the concourse. Tilwash seemed to have disappeared, but finally Haldar saw him on the far side of the concourse, speaking into some sort of comm as he walked. Haldar mingled with the people on the concourse, trying to get closer. Tilwash turned down one of the side passages, so Haldar sped up to try and catch up with him, but his path was blocked by a tech pushing some sort of fusion motor on a grav loader. He ducked behind that, but was then faced by a cheapjack selling radiation monitors from a carton marked 'Havadon Space Defence Force.' By the time Haldar reached the side passage, his prey had disappeared entirely.

Haldar shrugged. He'd done what he could. He glanced at his watch. He was running late. Toulis had left for his rendezvous well over an hour ago; Haldar suspected it was time he made his way back to the ship. He made his way back across the concourse where he was propositioned. First by a fearful and androgynous individual who was selling recreational narcotics; secondly by a thin girl who was selling herself to pay for them. The lifts weren't busy. Haldar travelled slowly down, all the while pondering on what he had overheard. He stepped off the lift when it got to the Serendipity's level and walked down the short passage. He was still lost in thought, but was suddenly aware of two men blocking the passage in front of him. The one in the front was tall and heavily built, wearing a one-piece workman's overall. The other, standing a little behind him, was shorter and stout. He wore a business suit which might have been smart on a thinner man who didn't sleep in it. It was the shorter man who addressed him.

"You Haldar Drom?"

Haldar decided that lying was unlikely to convince. "Yes."

"Mr Strang is wanting a word with you." The speaker supported his comment by gesturing with an energy pistol with a fanned nozzle.

Haldar raised both hands level with his head. "No need to point that at me. If Mr Strang wants a word, I am happy to go and see him." He turned, so he was standing sideways on to them. "Would one of you like to lead on?"

The man with the pistol muttered "Gorg, you lead, I'll follow and see there's no funny business."

The big man stepped forward. Haldar moved so that the thug was between him and the pistol and stabbed his fingertips at Gorg's eyes. His target lurched backwards and his colleague panicked and fired the pistol. Gorg screamed as the fan of energy sliced into his back. His colleague looked on, horrified, as his colleague, his body almost cut in half, fell to the floor. Then Haldar's clenched fist struck him on the temple. He collapsed on top of the twitching body. Haldar took a deep breath to recover his poise.

"They weren't very professional, were they?"

Haldar turned slowly. Behind him, watching, there stood another man, holding a ceramic handgun in each hand. Both were pointing at Haldar. Both had silencers.

"Mr Strang still wants to meet you. Apparently he isn't too bothered about your condition, provided you can still answer questions, so I suggest you be sensible and don't make trouble." He walked up to Haldar and, with one pistol always pointing at him, proceeded to pat him down.

"Turn round, slowly." Haldar did so. The gunman patted his back.

The man started backing away. "Follow me please, and keep the same distance."

Haldar gestured to the bodies on the floor. "What about the mess?"

The gunman laughed. "Kick the idiot with the gun he couldn't use."

Haldar prodded the top body with his foot. Eventually he was awarded with a groan.

"Rowjay, can you hear me?" the gunman barked.

The groaning got louder. "Rowjay, pull yourself together. I'm taking Mr Drom here to see Mr Strang; you clean up the mess before anyone asks questions. Got that?"

Rowjay pulled himself up into a kneeling position. The gunman awarded him a humourless smile. "Good; now get on with it. Drom, follow me."

Haldar wasn't led to the lifts, but through a door which led through a warren of service and maintenance bays and corridors. In one of the bays Haldar was allowed to overtake, and from then on he was guided by directions from behind.

Haldar arrived at a door which opened onto a broad corridor. He turned and looked over his shoulder. "Which way now?"

"Left."

Haldar stepped out into the corridor then stopped. "There's a man standing by a door along there."

"Journey's end; he's waiting for you."

Haldar walked towards the waiting man, who opened the door for him. He entered a bare chamber with four other doors off it. He stopped, not knowing which door to take. The other two came in behind him.

"The door on the left," the gunman advised.

Haldar stepped over to the door and opened in. As he did so he heard another door open. He glanced back to see Toulis step out.

Toulis spoke casually. "Good day all. Mr Strang is waiting. Hurry along." Then the tone of his voice changed, "Quick, stop him!"

Haldar, bemused, stopped as the two other men turned to look at him, guns raised. Toulis stepped behind them and raised his right hand. Haldar heard a soft 'splot' sound. It was repeated, and both men dropped. He found himself looking at Toulis over the bodies.

"What's going on Toulis?"

"No time for questions; take this." Toulis handed Haldar a small bladder with a nozzle. "The bladder you hold in the palm of your hand, the nozzle goes between your index finger and your middle finger. To fire it, just squeeze the bladder."

Haldar looked at the bladder, "What about just giving me a gun?"

"You can have a gun as well, but we've got to get your finger prints on this bladder, I cannot be found with it."

Haldar took the bladder and fitted it so it rested snug in his right hand. Toulis took the two pistols off the gunman and stuck them through the waist band of his britches. He handed the other guard's pistol to Haldar. "Swap jackets as well. If they just catch a quick glimpse of me, they might still think it's you. That way, it might just be possible to blame you and keep my nose clean."

Haldar took off his jacket. "It's pushing it, but I'm willing to give it a go."

Toulis shrugged on Haldar's jacket. "Do you know your way back to the Serendipity?"

Haldar stopped to go over the route in his mind. "I think so."

"Right, you get back, and I'll dispose of these two and follow you."

"Are they dead?"

"Oh yes, before they hit the ground. I wasn't risking these two remembering who helped you escape."

Haldar said, "Toulis, you just murdered two men."

Toulis kept his voice cheerful. "Alternatively, I've saved someone the cost of the executions, so it's probably more of a public service than murder."

Haldar glanced down at the bladder in his hand. His voice was cold when he asked, "Have you always carried one of these?"

Toulis stopped and faced him. "Look, Haldar. I know these people. I've never worked with them, but I've seen the results of their work. I decided to make sure you and I stayed alive, and to ensure that, I killed them as swiftly, silently and efficiently as I could. I do not regret it one bit. Now go before someone else turns up and I have to kill them as well."

Haldar, the pistol hidden inside the jacket he was now wearing, made his way back the way he came. The poison jabber he disposed of in a waste chute as he passed. He moved swiftly but with care, alert for sounds of pursuit. He was making his way along a short length of service corridor when a door ahead of him opened. Haldar reached for his pistol as Rowjay stepped out into the corridor. Rowjay saw him and hastily brought his handgun up as Haldar brought his own weapon up to bear. The heavy explosive slug hit Rowjay in the middle of the chest, shattering the sternum and blasting the heart and lungs clear out of the body cavity.

Haldar stepped carefully over the body. He hadn't time to waste. He crossed the freight route and came to the door leading to the Serendipity. He opened it. Patti was standing close by, covering the door with a heavy calibre projectile weapon, a model Haldar didn't immediately recognise. When she recognized him, she waved and lowered the barrel. "Where's Toulis?"

"Hopefully, he's coming. I'll wait for him; you go and make sure the ship is ready to leave."

"We're cleared to leave. We've even got the tube unbolted. All that's holding it is the sealant."

Haldar grimaced. "Not a comforting thought. Anyway, you go."

She gave him a mock salute and opened the door to the tube. She pulled it shut behind her, and was gone. Haldar opened the outer door again and looked down the Freight route. It was empty. He composed himself to wait. It was perhaps a quarter of an hour later when he heard something. He strained to hear. Yes, running feet. He brought the handgun up ready and waited. Suddenly Toulis burst out of a door, took cover behind the door frame and fired one of the pistols repeatedly in the direction he'd come from. Then he ran towards where Haldar stood. Haldar stepped aside and as Toulis threw himself through the door, Haldar started closing it and engaged all four emergency locks.

"No one will get through that without heavy cutting gear; you all right?"

Toulis picked himself off the floor and brushed himself down. "I see you met Rowjay."

"Yes, he tried to use that damned stupid broad aperture pistol on me."

Toulis tried to sound conciliatory. "Best end to him; he'd only have caused us trouble left alive, especially if he saw me."

Haldar gave a half smile. "Drawing a weapon on an armed police officer can carry the death sentence; anyway, I'm glad you've made it back. Were you recognized?"

Yes. I don't think they got a clear look at me."

"Yes? But you're shorter than me."

Toulis took off Haldar's jacket and ran his fingers over the back. "Here it is." He tugged and held his hand out to Haldar. "Tracking device; they'll have stuck that to you when they were searching you. When the technology says that the person they were chasing was you, who's going to argue with the technology?"

Toulis dropped the bug on the floor and ground it into the metal with his heel. "Let's leave."

*****

Ten minutes later, they were strapped into the acceleration couches and Serendipity was making its way out along the designated course towards the jump point from where it would be safe to enter hyperspace. Haldar brought Toulis up to date on all that had happened to him since the performance in the bar.

Toulis lay there, thinking about what he'd heard. Then he asked, "Did you hear much?"

"Not a lot. Sounded like Tilwash was trying to talk someone into some sort of scheme, one that would make a great deal of money."

"I know who that someone is," Toulis answered. "I recognized him as he went in. It was Little Kaidar, captain of the Falling Angel. He's one of Strang's captains, an out-and-out Starmancer, tends to be insubordinate, but popular among the more excitable captains."

Haldar turned towards the bridge and shouted. "Shilla, can you hear me?"

"Just about; you fed up of waiting for room service?"

"It's not that, it's just that I want to know how fast you can make it to Tsarina?"

"Is it urgent?"

"Yes."

"Well, if we don't stop off with cargo, and run with a higher G between jumps, we could shorten the trip. But it'll cost us money."

"The department will make up the difference."

Shilla laughed. "Can you bring Toulis into the conversation? He pays in cash, not vouchers."

Chapter 6

Taran lay on the floor of the cargo hold. The way the ship, the Falling Angel, was being buffeted on entry into atmosphere, it was the only practical alternative. Instinctively, he went through his pre-combat checklist.

Body armour comfortable? Check. Helmet fastened properly? He ran a finger under the strap, and it was firm rather than tight. Check. Head-up display working properly? Well, apart from the weather report section. That was projected onto the cracked part of his visor and was too blurred to read. He gave his helmet a sharp slap and the projection moved; now he could read the weather report, but couldn't see his current credit rating with the ship. He decided to settle with that. He glanced at the weather report, 'overcast, rain expected later.' Hopefully they wouldn't be there later. He checked through the rest of the head-up display.

Aerial photograph of combat zone? Check.

Mission timer? Check.

Recall Signal? It showed a steady green light rather than a red one, so should be OK. Check.

'Local Planetary Contact'? Some planets had one, most didn't. This was the contact number of someone who could be relied on to at least get you a lawyer. Taran was surprised to find that this planet had two, and one had 'new number' flashing in green next to it. He touched his throat mike and said quietly "Yarrow?"

"I have you, Taran." The voice of the Assault team leader cut through the static on his headset.

"Why two Local Planetary Contacts?"

There was a brief pause then Yarrow replied "for this trip, we have a different patron, and apparently this patron insists on us using his network."

"Thanks." Taran switched his throat mike off.

Ah well, call that a 'check'.

A new voice sounded in his ear. "Six minutes to combat zone and counting."

Taran started to check his energy carbine. The tell-tale on the power pack claimed it was fully charged and he ejected the pack and reloaded it to make sure the connections were good. He felt in his belt, confirming that he had his three spare power packs.

The voice in his ear spoke again.

"Five minutes to combat zone and counting. Ship board crew, count off by station."

Taran could hear familiar voices saying who they were and where they were.

He reached down and drew the heavy projectile pistol in the holster against his right thigh. Magazine fully loaded, spare magazine in holster, safety catch on. Check.

"Four minutes to combat zone and counting. Cargo crew count off."

These were the guys who would follow up behind the Assault team and shift the cargo into the hold. Hopefully, they wouldn't have to shoot anyone, just load.

Taran reached down and checked that his boot knife was still in its sheath. Check.

"Three minutes to combat zone and counting; Assault team count off."

Taran said his name after the guy on his left. He quite liked being in the Assault team. It was risky, but your job was to overwhelm the defence, then push out a perimeter. This meant that there was always the chance of that extra bit of loot, especially if the target security evaporated. Anything you got, you could keep; it was a perk of a dangerous job.

"Two minutes to combat zone and counting."

The ship was jinking now. Anyone who wasn't strapped into their action station would be lying on the floor.

"One minute to combat zone and counting."

Already the ramp in front of them was slowly opening. Taran glanced up and watched as the door gunner, snug in the cross harness which held him firmly to his seat, loaded the first round into the chamber and flicked the safety off. Through the gap left by the opening ramp, Taran could see trees flash past, then buildings. Finally, as the ship braked, there was just one large building. As the ship's landing pads touched the ground, he could see the building had a large door that was standing open with what appeared to be a security detail standing round the door.

The door gunner opened fire, and the heavy projectiles scythed into the men by the doorway. Taran was already running down the ramp, keeping to the right to avoid obscuring the door gunner. The gunner ceased fire, there were now too many of the Assault team moving out. Taran entered the building, the big warehouse they were told to secure. Someone came out of a small side office firing a handgun. Taran threw himself to one side, banging his helmet on the side of a packing case, but still managing to roll behind cover. One of his companions shot the man at close range. The team fanned out through the warehouse. Stacked here were a fair number of large packing cases—the Assault team had been briefed to be careful with these. Big dividing doors split it into bays, but they found the opening mechanism and the doors pulled back along their tracks. The other bays were empty.

Over his headset Taran heard the assault commander report that the area was secure. Back came the order they had been waiting for. Push out into town, expand the perimeter, and get rich. Cheering, the men of the Assault team left the warehouse to the cargo crew and spread out through the nearest houses.

*****

Every so often you get one of the good jobs, Willon decided. A few days ago, he had swapped his day off with one of the other journalists who wanted a day's fishing, and so Willon was in the office when this job came in. He still wasn't sure how exactly he'd managed to get it, but he suspected being the junior left in the office when everyone else took a long lunch helped. Hence, when the call came in, he was the only one available. Consequently, he was the one they'd sent out from Kaunas City to cover the annual Kenehan swimwear pageant. The girls would promenade along a flower-bedecked walkway on the banks of the Colitas River, and the winner would get some suitable prize. Willon felt that the real winner would be the Kenehan Marketing Authority which would doubtless be ready to make the best of any publicity the pageant brought them. That, Willon felt, was probably fair.

He checked out his camera, zooming in and out. It was the first time they'd issued him with one with a 'planetary coverage' satellite link, and he was still a little nervous of it. He checked the light levels. Pity about the cloud cover, the tech staff would have to dub in sunshine later. He looked round and focussed on a tree-rat that was sitting on a branch, chittering at its mate, who was peering at him out of a hole in the Baol tree. The tree-rat bounded out along the branch, picked a blossom and carried it back, still chittering. The female crept out of the hole, grabbed the blossom and scurried back to the hole with it. The male sat there, watching the hole, grooming its whiskers before finally sauntering to the hole and disappearing after its mate. The mixing desk would love that one.

The Kaunas City office came back to him on his headset; the satellite link was working smoothly, and they were already mixing the holo. Willon let the camera play along the river, building up stock footage for the background. Then he saw something coming up river. He zoomed in on it, and to his astonishment it was a starship, barely skimming the water. He broke in to the banal chatter coming from the office.

"Do you see what I'm seeing? Spaceship at below treetop height."

"Lock on that ship, keep tracking. This could be more interesting than the pageant."

"Thanks, people."

Willon glanced round, looking at the laser towers. There was six of them, deathly white and etiolated ceramic extrusions; each with a bulbous and transparent gun cupola on the top. They were there to prevent exactly this sort of incident. The one nearest to him stirred, the gunner was obviously awake. The heat scarred 'barrel' of the laser was starting to track the ship; it opened fire and emitted a brief flash of light before going dead. Willon glanced at the other towers, they too were still. From below him, he could hear someone shouting at the girls to run for the woods. Obviously someone feared slavers. He was starting to feel exposed. He set the camera on the mount, locked it onto the ship and then he dropped to the ground. Here professional curiosity battled with common sense, and rather than following the girls into the woods, he made his way back into the town.

The ship had landed next to the big warehouse by the river. Willon pulled the backup camera out of the pocket sewn for it in his jacket and checked it out. This one had no satellite link, but he could link it through the other camera later. It was about this point he realised someone was screeching at him through his head piece.

"I'm listening, but please keep your voice down."

"What's going on there?

Willon was jogging down the side street, against a flow of people fleeing the town. His answer was uneven.

"I'd say Starmancer attack. The towers are out; I've got footage of people fleeing."

He turned around, panning the camera. The houses were wooden framed and wooden panelled, all intricately worked, the panels were apprentice pieces done by people long dead.

Willon moved more cautiously now, feeling conspicuous as he was entirely on his own. He turned the next corner very carefully and found himself looking straight down the road at the Starmancer ship. It had the hold doors open. A cargo handler trundled down the ramp of the ship on ligni-steel tracks and into the warehouse; two men were dragging bodies out of the way and stacking them to one side. The headset was still chattering at him, but he ignored it. He peered carefully through the camera view-finder and focused, adjusting his stance to get the best camera angle. The headset was shrieking at him, so finally he switched it off, the noise level was just too high. The cargo handler made three runs, loaded high with crates, but he also saw the Starmancers fanning out. Three moved down the road towards him. At that point, he realised he'd moved away from the wall for a better shot. He glanced round hastily and saw an open doorway and dived for it. There were shouts down the street and he scrambled to his feet and ran through the house, out of the back, only to find himself in another open lane leading down to the ship. He kept running, went through the next house, this time shutting the elaborately carved door behind him. He was almost too late; something punched a hole the size of his fist in the door, at head height.

He ran through the house, opened the back door, to see another street, but then darted upstairs, leaving the door hanging open. Below him he heard the front door crash open and there were voices below. Their accent was strange, their talk staccato. One shouted that he could see nothing out of the back door, another was apparently opening cupboards, the third announced he was going to see if there was anything worth having upstairs. Willon looked around the small, over-furnished bedroom for somewhere to hide. He couldn't see anywhere that wouldn't be searched by an enthusiastic looter. So, for lack of a better option, he stood behind the door holding a heavy chamber pot, ready to club anyone coming into the room. The footsteps on the stairs stopped and someone shouted something about a recall, and the three Starmancers left. Willon went to the window and watched them running down the street back to the ship. He leaned against the window, the tension of the last few minutes slowly draining out of him. 'Gods,' he thought to himself, 'that was far too close.' Standing up, he made his way back down to the front door. The street was empty, but around the ship there was frantic activity. The cargo loader was abandoned and the ship took off even as the cargo hold doors were closing. Then, even over the sound of the Starmancer's engines, Willon could hear a deeper roar. He glanced up and a large warship was slowly descending towards them out of the cloud. He could see the bright flashes as its laser batteries opened up. The Starmancer's ship was moving away, towards the river, firing back. A house at the end of the street disappeared in a beam of light. Willon, temporarily blinded, threw himself down onto the ground and felt the earth quivering beneath him. As he concentrated on controlling his bladder, the noise above him moved to his right, and then there was an explosion. Even sheltered by the houses, he felt the blast. The Starmancer must have exploded low over the river. A warm rain fell briefly around him. As the noise died away, he stood up, a little unsteadily, and looked up. The warship was climbing steadily; it was almost out of sight. Willon brushed himself off and checked his camera. He had already decided that he was going to check out the situation before he switched his headset back on.

*****

Taran had got ahead of the rest of the Assault team—experience had taught him that the best pickings were in private houses well away from Industrial buildings. He'd studied the satellite imagery on his head-up display and had guessed that there were some desirable houses scattered among woodland, a quarter of a mile from where the ship would come down.

The houses he jogged past were all deserted, sometimes with their doors hanging open as the inhabitants had fled. He moved the ear-jacks from his helmet comm so they didn't interfere with his hearing, and picked a house to loot. It stood back from the road among trees. Indeed, at first glance, it might have been mistaken for a copse of Honey-jar trees, their grossly bulbous trunks planted too close together so their trunks had fused. Closer inspection showed that one of the trunks sported a door, coffin-shaped and intricately carved, while in the few gaps between the trunks there were irregularly shaped windows.

Taran approached the door with care, opened it and stood silently, listening, his finger still on the trigger of his energy carbine. After two or three minutes he allowed himself to relax. There was no one about, so he made his way upstairs. He checked that the upstairs was also empty before starting to methodically search the house. In the master bedroom he found jewellery tucked at the back of a drawer full of ladies' underwear. In what might have been an office he found a cash box, and what appeared to be the wage packets of a dozen employees. He opened one of the wage packets. Obviously, this world used Thalian Credits, as did most of the rest of the sector. He dropped the packets into a pouch on his belt.

A tell-tale was flashing on his head-up display. He glanced at it. It came from the crack on his visor. For some reason, his ship credit had gone below zero. He mentally shrugged and carried on searching; he could sort that out with the paymaster when he got back. Then, in a moment of panic, he refocused properly on the display. The ship credit figure was there, and was comfortably positive. He slapped his helmet with his left hand, and the projection shifted. It was the recall signal that was flashing red. He must have jarred the helmet when he'd dodged in the warehouse. He hastily popped the ear-jacks back. The recall was sounding. Cursing again, he ran down the stairs and out through the open front door. Ahead of him he could see the Falling Angel rise off the ground, with the great bulk of the Taurus hanging there high above it. The Falling Angel jinked, attempted to avoid the incoming laser beams, and disappeared from his sight up river. Suddenly there was a bright flash of light and an explosion.

The Falling Angel was no more.

Taran stood there, stunned; his headset suddenly silent, the head-up display frozen at the last download. He was on his own, and retribution would not be long in arriving. He gazed round. Next to the house was a sunken garden. The bottom was paved with stone slabs. On three sides of the banks, as they ran down to the stone paving, were a riot of flowers. On the fourth side there was a sheer face with a large double door set into it; a garage? Taran walked down a narrow, paved stair and opened the door. There sat a flitter, a luxury model, sleek, predatory, ultramarine with excessive chrome trim. He climbed into the seat and powered it up. On initial checks, it looked promising. He went back into the house and went up to the master bedroom. He stripped and dressed hurriedly in clothes he took from the wardrobe. After some thought he put his helmet and body armour back on, as well as the boots. The previous owner had narrow feet, and none of the shoes would fit.

Resplendent in borrowed finery, matching tunic and trews in bottle green with lace edging, Taran made his way back to the flitter. Admittedly, the body armour, utility belt and helmet were incongruous, but he would worry about that later. He opened the garage doors wide, climbed into the flitter, fired up the engines and flew it out into the open. Checking the satellite image on this frozen head-up display, he headed out of town at just above treetop height.

*****

Haldar was riding in the suborbital belonging to the Governor's Dignity Battalion. He had landed on Tsarina barely four hours before, and had gone to his office. He'd submitted his report to the Governor in person. Vladimir had listened to his verbal account in grim silence. Haldar had long ago classified the Governor as essentially 'a nice guy', but no towering genius. Still it was obvious Vladimir had worked out the implications for himself. The interview was still in progress when reports had come in of a Starmancer attack on the town of Kenehan. The Dignity Battalion was scrambled as the nearest unit, and Haldar hitched a lift. The infantry were going there to help pick up the pieces and keep order, so it made sense to travel with them. Not only that, but he'd probably have to rely on them for support if his investigations started irritating people, so it might be wise to have them at his side as soon as possible.

He joined the company's officers in the suborbital's bridge for the briefing and watched the hologram of the attack, letting Captain Gillik talk them through it.

Gillik was a short, thickset man, laconic and reputed to have a dry sense of humour. He was also very experienced, and Haldar was interested to see what he made of the action captured by the hologram.

Gillik pressed a button and the hologram spluttered into life with the sound turned low so they could hear Gillik's voice.

"Here the correspondent is filming the preparation for the annual Kenehan swimwear pageant. At any moment, we will see the assembled local lovelies. Ah, I'm glad that woke you up, Lieutenant, just in time for the camera to pan down river. Yes, there you see it, the Starmancers' ship coming upriver, and keeping below treetop height. The naval people tell me that it is about the size of a large frigate. Yes, the camera has panned back to the girls, and the organisers are telling them to make a run for the trees. At this point, I think they may have feared a slave raid. Ah, did you notice that? The laser tower is coming to life. Someone has woken the occupant and he has switched over to manual. See, it traverses, he aims, fires, and there is a brief burst of power before the system goes down. This happened to all six towers." Gillik took a sip from his glass before continuing. "Our correspondent has obviously set the camera on automatic and it is continuing to film. But now the Starmancers have landed right by the warehouse. There appears to be some sort of shoot-out, but we cannot really see it, and here we see them as they are hastily loading the contents into their ship." Gillik moved his finger on the controls, "I'll fast-forward this bit; if you want the pleasure of watching men working frantically for about fifteen minutes, then you can either announce a snap inspection of the barracks, or alternatively come back and watch the holo later. Ah yes, here we are; suddenly there appears to be some sort of recall. Some of the Starmancers have been spreading out to loot the town as well, and here we can see men running frantically for their ship. See, it is powering up; you can see from the haze around it that it has even raised its shields. And now the dénouement, gentlemen. We have the Taurus."

At this point, Haldar could hear gasps from some of the men around him, but Gillik kept on speaking.

"Yes, I know she is one big mother, and yes, I didn't expect her so deep into atmosphere. See, she is opening up with her light laser batteries. The Starmancer is firing back, and he is going out along the river, out of sight now, but the Taurus is still firing, and yes, here it ends."

As Gillik went quiet, the hologram flashed white. The Starmancer ship had died.

Gillik switched off the hologram and turned to his assembled officers.

"We have among us Haldar Drom of the Governor's Investigation Office. We will be working with him, so I wonder if you would care to say anything, Officer Drom."

Haldar grimaced as he heard the old title. He stood up and looked around before speaking.

"Firstly, I'd like to thank Captain Gillik for the lift. My department is awfully slow at paying travel expenses." He let them chuckle over the old joke and then continued. "Secondly, we will be the first people in. There may be Starmancers about who didn't make it to their ship. They will be armed and they will be dangerous, but they might also make good witnesses, so I'd be grateful if you could take prisoners." He glanced round and was glad to see that none of them thought this was an unrealistic request.

"I'd also be glad to be kept in the loop if any of your boys spots anything untoward. But," and here he glanced towards Gillik, "in this situation, I know you have your own job to do and I don't want to get in the way."

At this point he was saved from further discussion by the pilot, who called for Captain Gillik. Gillik went forward and stood by the pilot, studying the landing displays.

"Problem?"

"Not as such," said the pilot, "but those laser towers are live."

Gillik studied the display. "They must have got them back on-line. It is three hours after the raid."

"I've asked them to shut them down to allow us in, but I've got no response so far, sir."

Gillik reached for the handset. "I'll talk to them. Put me through, please."

"You're through, sir."

"Hello, this is Captain Gillik, Reaction Company, in the Suborbital. We request the Laser towers be shut down so we can land."

Gillik took the headset off the pilot and appeared to be listening to someone. He replied.

"No, that will not happen. We are not going to make an approach with the towers live."

The voice obviously continued, but Gillik spoke over it.

"The option is yours. We will land in seven minutes. If the towers are not off-line in three minutes we will have the Taurus melt them from orbit."

Gillik switched off the handset and passed the headset back to the pilot who was still watching the display.

"Towers powered down, sir."

Gillik allowed himself a brief smile. "Continue with the approach and bring us down near the river, but clear of where the Starmancer landed. I don't want to spoil a crime scene."

Gillik turned to his assembled officers. "Landing in seven minutes, assume presence of hostile forces, but do not open fire unless we are actively attacked. We're here to rescue people, not kill them. That being said, we hit the ground ready for combat."

*****

The 'assault landing' was straight out of the textbook. Admittedly, few such landings are filmed by a waiting journalist, but the platoons ignored him as they fanned out. Most other-ranks learn early on in their careers the wisdom of leaving talking to the media to someone else. Finally Willon noticed two officer types walking towards him, so after ensuring that they had been captured on camera, he switched it off and waited. As they got within conversational distance, he decided to be helpful. In this policy he felt actively encouraged by the presence of the security detail. Disturbingly muscular and heavily armed individuals seemed to be closing in on him from all sides.

"Gentlemen, I am Willon Cartif, of Tsarina Broadcasting, Channel Six." He then added in a quieter voice, "I've got the camera switched off, but you'll have to give me a minute to shut down the headset."

It was Gillik who answered, "don't worry, Mr Cartif; we've been jamming all transmissions since we landed." Gillik then glanced at Haldar. "I think this one is your problem." He turned back to Willon. "I'd be grateful if we could have a copy of your film of our landing, I'd like to take the men through it at the debrief; it's good to check for errors in operational procedure; anyway, a good day to you."

Gillik and his security detail headed towards the warehouse, leaving Haldar with Willon.

Haldar weighed up the younger man. Mid-twenties, sharp but lacking the air of world weary cynicism so many journalists seemed to affect. "You're the reporter who filmed the raid?"

Willon nodded.

Haldar smiled to reassure the younger man. "A nice bit of work. Come, walk me through it, and you can show me any other footage you have as well." Willon looked a little uncertain, so Haldar added, "I'm Haldar Drom of the Governor's Investigation Office."

Willon looked even more uncertain, and gestured at the fatigues Haldar was currently wearing. "I thought this was a military operation. GIO means it's political, and way above my level."

Haldar put a companionable arm around the younger man's shoulders. "Well, I still hold military rank, if it cheers you up. Let's go to where you started filming from."

Haldar let Willon lead him to where the camera had been first set up, and then they walked together, retracing the route Willon had followed, towards the warehouse. They stopped occasionally to study the footage on Willon's back-up camera, but eventually they arrived at the warehouse.

People were making their way back into town. By the time Haldar and Willon arrived at the warehouse, the bodies were being loaded onto a six-wheeled cargo hauler by a squad of soldiers detailed to the job, while two men in civilian clothes were fussing with mops, trying to clean up the blood that had pooled on the concrete floor. Gillik was talking to several elderly men who seemed particularly animated. Gillik was taking notes, and glanced up when Haldar and Willon arrived.

"These gentlemen are members of the Board of Assessors. Apparently, the warehouse has been virtually emptied." Gillik nodded towards a stack of twenty crates sitting forlornly in the echoing empty space of the warehouse. "They are what's left."

One of the Assessors stepped forward as spokesman. He wore a pair of bib and brace overalls suitable to a working man. Yet the overalls, while made of heavy serge, were richly patterned, using minute glass beads in a score of colours.

"I am Assessor Borne of the Guild of Marquetry Inlayers. A couple of weeks ago the warehouse management and security team sent a message round to all the guilds, telling us that the warehouse was virtually full. Therefore arrangements were made to summon an appropriate haulier to transport the contents directly off planet to our agents."

"Does all Kenehan furniture pass through this warehouse?"

"Yes." Assessor Borne was emphatic. "It all passes through this warehouse, and is sold through the Kenehan Marketing Authority. Each workshop is inspected regularly to ensure that only work of the right quality is produced and sold. Inferior pieces are burned in the presence of the inspector. Pieces considered adequate are transported directly to the warehouse."

Haldar looked round the empty warehouse and gestured to some empty crates.

"Are they standard sized crates?"

"Yes, everything we produce can fit into standard crates. Only the bigger pieces need to be disassembled."

"What about fire precautions?"

Assessor Borne pointed to tracks in the floor. "The warehouse is built of a dozen standard *pre-cast* sections." Haldar thought he could hear distain in the craftsman's voice. A craftsman and artist, the Assessor was never going to approve of anything mass-produced. "Each pre-cast section can be separated from the next by panels which move along the rails. The Starmancers obviously rolled them back to get access to all twelve bays."

Haldar examined the panels carefully. Thanks to Bartan, he knew that someone other than Kenehan Marketing Authority was selling Kenehan-made furniture and was using it to smuggle Abate. It struck him that the warehouse might be the place the furniture had been taken from, perhaps with the collusion of the guards.

"And when you were here last, the panels were in place."

Assessor Borne nodded. "Yes, I saw the first bay filled and the panels closed. I haven't been back since, but it is standard procedure to fill a bay and close it off."

"And when a bay is closed off, it is not possible to see what is in it?" Haldar's question was casual.

“No, the seal is good and the material is not transparent.”

”And there is no other way into the warehouse?”

“Access to the wharf is normally though Bay One at the far end, nearest the river. If anything does go out by river, it would leave by that door. But when the freighter lands, we tend to use both doors to empty the warehouse. This entrance tends to be used purely for filling the warehouse. It’s handy for the clerk’s office and for logging things in.”

Haldar smiled his understanding and thanked the Assessor for his information. Beckoning to Willon, they went deep into the warehouse.

“Willon, I’m afraid I’m going to have to conscript you into the Governor’s Investigation Office.”

“Can I decline?”

Haldar thought briefly, “in theory, you can appeal to the Emperor in person.”

Willon appeared bemused. “But the Empire fell two hundred years ago.”

“I did say in theory.” Haldar tried to sound conciliatory. “Think about it this way; you get paid a day rate which is probably better than what you’re getting at work, and your employer will be ‘encouraged’ to keep paying you.”

“But I’m a journalist, what about the story?”

“Ah, there I can put your mind at rest. Any film released will be credited to you; you’re the definitive ‘man on the spot.’ Obviously there could be things you cannot mention, but generally we compensate you for the loss of one story by passing you another at some point in the future.”

“I’ll do it.”

“Ah, it’s nice to deal with a reasonable man.” Haldar fished around in his pocket and pulled out an ID card. “Thumb print there please, to activate it. Yes, after peeling off the strip.” He watched as Willon applied his thumb. “Congratulations, you’re now Officer Cartif of the Governor’s Investigation Office. Technically, that makes you the same rank as me, but we know you’re not. The infantry will doubtless obey your orders, sergeants will do so in a way that implies you’re an idiot, but they do that with everyone. The lieutenants will probably obey you if what you’re saying sounds reasonable. With Captain Gillik restrict yourself to polite requests.” He paused. “Understood?”

“Yes,” Willon said. “Do I salute you?”

“Only on pay parades.”

Haldar led Willon towards the far end of the warehouse, where they could inspect the wharf-side door. Haldar examined it carefully.

“The main door here hasn’t been opened for some time, but there is a smaller inspection door here which is well oiled and is obviously the one most used.”

"Do you think that is how the crates were taken out?"

"Well, your film footage showed that the Starmancers were lucky if they got away with much more than thirty. So I'm assuming someone else took them. So just a preliminary thought … You've seen the crates, the door is certainly wide enough to get a crate through. You couldn't shift them quickly, but perhaps someone was taking out a crate a day, every day, and was shipping them out constantly. I'd say most crates could be manhandled by three or four men."

Willon glanced round the now empty warehouse. "Didn't they have security?"

"Yes, it was provided by a company based in the capital, Liadan Consolidated Securities, or LCS."

"Where are their employees now?"

Haldar gestured towards the other door, "Did you notice the bodies that were being loaded onto the carrier?"

Willon was troubled. "So any witnesses are dead."

"Perhaps." Haldar then changed tack. "How much do you know about Kenehan?"

"Other than that they have an annual swimwear pageant?"

"Yes, although that was a new one to me."

"Well," said Willon, thoughtfully, "They do a lot with furniture, very high quality furniture, and other woodwork. I think I'm right in saying that the place is run by a collection of guilds, each headed by an Assessor, and the Assessor is generally the finest craftsman in the guild, at least in the eyes of his peers."

"Very good; I'd say Assessor Borne gives the impression of being a good example of his type: very much the craftsman, not taking too much notice of the paperwork, except when his money is concerned."

"Yes, and isn't everything sold though the Kenehan Marketing Authority?"

Haldar looked thoughtful. "Technically it is, and as Assessor Borne said, when the warehouse is about full, the KMA makes arrangements for the goods to be shipped out. Yet we know that, off-world, an organisation called the Kenehan Independent Traders is also selling the furniture, or was until it was busted for smuggling drugs."

Haldar waved an arm around the massive empty space of the warehouse.

"You filmed the Starmancers loading. On the film the cargo-handler makes three trips, perhaps five crates a trip. Allow another three at the most for the time you weren't able to film, so say that's six trips. How many crates will this place hold?"

Willon shrugged. "A thousand, maybe more?"

"It was full, they took out thirty crates, and there are now twenty left. Where are the other nine hundred and fifty crates?"

"So what do you suspect?"

Haldar rubbed his face with his hand. "Right, let's set out the pieces of the jigsaw and see if we can see a picture. Firstly, Kenehan Independent Traders has been acquiring furniture. From what I've been told, it wouldn't be easy for them to get the furniture from the craft workshops; everything is inspected. But if they put their people into the warehouse ... ?"

Here he shot a glance at Willon to see if the young journalist was following him. Willon nodded.

Haldar continued, "secondly, I suspect that someone, probably KIT, took the other crates." He paused, and looked round the warehouse. "So how did they get nearly a thousand crates out without anyone noticing?" Haldar took his hat off and ran his fingers through his short cropped hair. "So, perhaps this happened over a period of years, quietly fiddling the books so that no one noticed. Hmmm, perhaps the guilds were in on it to an extent, siphoning some off to KIT because it gave a better margin."

Willon asked, "and the drugs?"

Haldar stopped half way through putting his hat back on. "I don't think the guilds were in on the drug side of it; too much of a risk to their reputation. But there again, greed makes respectable people do the most *interesting* things." Haldar put his cap back on. "But at some point there might have to be an audit, and they had to explain away where all the furniture was. Much to their joy, the Starmancers arrived and inadvertently took the blame for the real thieves."

Willon was silent for a while. "But they couldn't hope for Starmancers to spontaneously decide to attack ... ." He stopped speaking as realisation dawned on him. "Ah. You think that whoever it is invited the Starmancers in?"

Haldar straightened his cap a little more and said, "We haven't had a Starmancer attack on the planet for seventeen years." Here Willon noticed the pride in Haldar's voice. Haldar glanced at his watch and added, "We have someone to see. I asked Captain Gillik to have a weapons technician check the towers out. On top of that, there's another question; What on earth was the Taurus doing? She doesn't come into the Tsarina's atmosphere every decade! Yet, she just happens to turn up within half an hour of the Starmancers." Haldar unnecessarily adjusted his hat. "I just love it when you get too many coincidences. Anyway, let's find the weapons technician."

Haldar led the young journalist out of the warehouse and looked round for Captain Gillik. The captain was talking to a growing number of civilians and was starting to appear harassed. Haldar decided to leave him to it, and then saw the man he was looking for. He tapped Willon on the shoulder.

"There he is; follow me."

Haldar set off across the grass to where the weapon tech was working on a trooper's energy lance. He saw Haldar and Willon approaching, so stood up and saluted smartly. Haldar saluted back.

"They said you were busy in there sir, so I thought I'd wait here until you were free."

"Fair enough, soldier," Haldar replied. "What did you find?"

"All six laser towers had undergone routine maintenance a week ago. All six had had their main fuses overhauled, and in every case the fuse was stripped down and the core was replaced by a standard household core. That's why the crews got them back on line so quickly. They just had to put in a new fuse from the stores. Only the stores were locked on the grounds that it was a holiday, what with the pageant and everything."

"Thank you, soldier," Haldar smiled briefly at him, "most useful."

He turned to Willon. "Could you check out who controlled access to stores please? I want to talk to Kaunas City, and the only way I'll get through the jamming is to use the Suborbital's radio. I'll meet you by your first camera position in half an hour."

*****

When Haldar got to the rendezvous point, Willon was already waiting. The young journalist had the air of a man modestly pleased with himself. So much so that he almost blurted out his information before Haldar reached him.

"I was chatting to one of the men in the laser towers. He was keen to know what was going on down here, so was pleased to talk to someone who could tell him. LCS controls the stores. Apart from that, the towers are each manned on a rota, everyone between twenty and sixty is on it, but you can trade shifts. This means it tends to be older men who do the job, keeps them out of the house. The towers were paid for by funds generously donated by a consortium of river ferries. At their insistence, they are fitted with dead-man switches so they will open fire on anything above treetop height unless countermanded. That's why there's no scheduled air services here and even private flitters go out along the river at low altitude."

"I hadn't realised it was that bad," Haldar said thoughtfully. "No wonder Gillik wanted them powered down before he came within their range." Haldar was silent for a moment and then asked, "who does the maintenance, then?"

"LCS has the contract, and LCS tends to supply spares."

"Do we see a picture emerging?" Haldar commented. "Now I'd like to watch that film of yours again."

"Will playing it as a 2D projection on the camera viewfinder be good enough?"

"Probably." Haldar watched as Willon adjusted the camera.

Willon stepped back. "You'll probably have to squat down here to see it properly, but it'll give you the same view that I had as the film was being shot."

Haldar squatted down as he'd been instructed and watched the film.

"Stop it ... now."

Willon reached forward and pressed a button.

Haldar pointed to the picture. "See? Here, as you pan across, the ship hasn't appeared yet; but study the warehouse."

Willon peered closely. "The door is open and there are five, perhaps six men sitting about by it."

"Can you zoom in?"

Haldar watched as the figures grew larger. "Yes, there they are, the security team provided by LCS, all present and waiting."

"But if they were waiting to assist the Starmancers, why did the Starmancers kill them?"

"Perhaps someone wanted to dispose of all witnesses, Willon. So far there is a distinct shortage of witnesses. All the LCS security team are dead, all the Starmancers are dead."

There was a bleeping from Haldar's jacket pocket. He pulled out a compact phone. "Excuse me a minute .... Haldar here."

He listened for a while and then said "and where is it now?" There was a further period of listening and Haldar asked "survivors?" He listened a while longer and finally said "thank you," and shut the phone.

"Sorry about that. Kaunas City can get through to me, but I cannot get through to them. Before, when talking to them, I asked if there was a regular ferry or boat service going through. There are several up and down the river and one is run by LCS. However, LCS shut down the ferry service last week."

"Did they say why?" Willon managed to inject a considerable degree of cynicism into the question.

"The ferry, a small cargo and passenger vessel, was lost with all hands when it was seen to go out of control and collide with the pier. At that point the cargo, which appears to have been listed as 'organic solvents', burned explosively."

"Should have stuck with furniture; it might be a bit on the heavy side, but the biggest risk is dropping it on your foot," Willon said. Then he added, "I'm glad I'm not their insurer."

"That was the other thing I was about to tell you. There is an Insurance Loss Adjuster coming out on a private flight. I think he might want a word with us."

*****

Haldar decided at this point that rank ought to have some privileges. He had not eaten for longer than he cared to remember and when quizzed, Willon admitted he too had missed at least one meal. By now most of the population were back in town, so leaving a soldier to wait for the incoming flight, they went to find a restaurant that was open. At the corner of Mire Lane and Lesser Sump they found a small eatery where they dined on small, wine-fried river fish. The fish were accompanied and complemented by a bowl of boiled parsnips served with a sauce of celery seed, rue, honey, pepper, raisin wine, stock and a little olive oil. They had just opened a bottle of wine when a soldier arrived, accompanied by a man who was at least middle-aged, wearing the dress of a successful businessman, a nondescript suit with long tunic and trousers flared slightly from the knee. He nodded to Haldar when he entered, and Haldar gestured to a third chair at their table. Then Haldar asked the soldier, "have you eaten yet?"

"No sir."

Haldar walked to the counter, cut a generous slice of meat pie, placed it on a plate and handed it to him.

The soldier looked surprised but took the plate. "Thank you sir," he said, and left before anyone could change his mind.

Haldar bowed formally to their bemused hostess. "Please put that on my bill, and we'll have another glass for my friend." He glanced at the Loss Adjuster. "Have you eaten?"

"A slice of pie wouldn't hurt, cut like you did for my guide, if you don't mind."

Haldar placed the rest of the pie on a plate in front of him and sat down. "There you are, Toulis; enjoy."

"You know him?" Willon asked.

Toulis grinned over a forkful of pie, "you might say that."

Willon looked askance at Haldar, who glared meaningfully at their hostess standing by the counter. Somewhat flustered, she retreated to the kitchen, shutting the door behind her. Haldar took his phone out of his pocket and placed it on the table. He pressed a couple of buttons and it started to play rather jingly folk music. He leaned back in his chair and said, "even if she does fancy eavesdropping she'll struggle to hear over that."

He reached forward, took the bottle and poured wine into three glasses, and then passed them round the table. Finally, he answered Willon's question.

"Yes, I know him. Toulis Hart works for Trans-world (Tsarina) Insurance. I'd suggest that it is considered a reputable firm which covers goods in transit, merchant vessels of all sorts and is the first port of call for anyone wanting to insure large, valuable cargo."

Toulis, his mouth full, merely nodded his agreement, so Haldar continued.

"It must be said that it is not entirely obvious who the real owners of this company are, but when you work your way back through various shell companies and similar, it is surprising how often the name of Waylan Strang comes up."

"Waylan Strang? Isn't he the Starmancer?" Willon asked.

At this point Toulis felt obliged to chip in, and swallowed. "Alleged Starmancer." Having mounted a token defence of his employer, he continued with mock pomposity, "I have been told that Mr Strang is a martyr to space sickness and rarely leaves his native world."

Haldar replied with specious formality. "I think I can assert that Mr Strang has never been proven in court to have personally taken part in any piratical operation, saving such that are the normal part and parcel of the insurance and banking industry." Haldar took another sip of wine and continued. "Mr Strang needs some way to invest his money. I had thought that the professions of Insurer and Starmancer should fit well together. You'd think it would help you keep the premiums competitive, but I'm reliably informed that there are far too many up-and-coming Starmancers out there." He turned to Toulis and asked "how much was the warehouse insured for?"

"If I was to tell you that we work on the principle that each case is worth an average of twelve thousand Thalian Credits, would you believe me?"

"Each case is three years' wages?" Willon asked.

Toulis allowed himself a dry smile, "I'd have said nearer two, but you can see where I'm coming from. The cargo was worth more than the ship that was destroyed."

"Just out of idle curiosity, to whom did the Starmancer ship belong?" Willon asked.

"It was the 'Falling Angel,' captained by a gentleman called Little Kaidar. To speak frankly, as between professionals, it was owned, indirectly, by Wayland Strang. Perhaps it is better to use the Starmancer term and say that Mr Strang was the patron."

Haldar chuckled and then recovered his composure. "So let me get this right. someone has hit Mr Strang for an insurance claim of over twelve million Thalian Credits, and at the same time has managed to cost him a ship worth nearly as much."

"Not to mention that it appears that LCS is comprehensively insured with us," Toulis volunteered. "I have a bill on my desk for a ferry destroyed in a freak harbour accident, and I have no doubt the security men killed in the raid will have been insured with us, too, so we will have to pay out to their dependents."

There was silence and then Willon asked quietly, "does Wayland Strang know this?"

"Not yet, the news cannot travel faster than the spaceship carrying the news. If he is still at Havadon Higher Orbital, it will take three weeks for the news to reach him. If he's travelling, or further away, it could take longer."

"Won't he hear faster than having a message travel by ordinary commercial shipping?" Willon asked.

"To the best of my knowledge, he has no special messengers based on Tsarina. Indeed why should he? Dedicated message carriers are expensive, and Tsarina is the far end of nowhere. He'll not find out until the first report reaches him, placed by my office on an ordinary merchant ship."

"So what will he do when he finds out?"

Toulis considered his words carefully. "He will not be entirely happy. Indeed, he was not happy before; now, he might be angry enough to do something foolish."

Haldar spoke, obviously picking his words carefully. "It strikes me that, at this point, our organisations' desires continue to run in parallel for some distance."

Toulis nodded. "Yes, I think we can work on this one together."

Willon was somewhat bemused. "But I thought that Wayland Strang had his ship raid Tsarina?"

Haldar and Toulis glanced at each other, and Haldar answered the young journalist. "No, a ship in some way owned by Wayland Strang raided Tsarina, or more particularly it raided Kenehan, on the planet of Tsarina. But I'm not entirely sure how many ships Mr Strang has. If you were to ask whether Mr Strang knew about this raid, I'd say he didn't."

Here he glanced at Toulis, who said "on a day to day basis, I suspect that Wayland Strang isn't too certain how many ships he owns, controls or directs. In this matter, I would suggest that my principal should be regarded in the same light as a shipping line. For core work, the line has its own ships, but it will often use subcontractors and similar for jobs that are peripheral to the core business. In this case, someone who we might wish to call a subcontractor overstepped the mark. They took on what they thought could well be a lucrative job without first checking with the principal. Of course, we now know who suborned Little Kaidar." He looked at his audience, to see if they were following him and then continued. "We need to find out more about LCS, and I'd also like to find the missing crates. They represent approximately twelve million Thalian Credits, and our company can do without paying out sums like that."

Willon said "if they were used to smuggle drugs, won't they already be dispersed?"

"Probably," Toulis conceded, "but there might still be some in stock on the planet, and these I want to find."

Haldar had been listening, and then he said "we need a word with the Captain of the Taurus, if only to find out why he just happened to appear on the scene when he did."

Toulis finished his wine. "What if I take Willon here back to Kaunas City and see if we can discover more details about LCS and locate the missing furniture? You go and have a quiet word with the Navy. I'm sure they'll be far more open with you than with me."

Haldar emptied his glass. "Seems like a plan. While you're travelling it might be a good idea to explain to Willon what has happened since we met in the Border Kingdoms. I'll go and have a word with Captain Gillik, see if he'll let me borrow the suborbital. It can go up and the Taurus can come down to join us. I'm sure she's still lurking up there." He pushed the chair back and stood up. "We'll probably meet in Kaunas City."

He pocketed his phone, turned and walked out of the door, closing it gently behind him. Toulis finished the last of his pie at about the same time the proprietor reappeared behind the counter. "I hope you notice what the sly bastard has done," Toulis muttered to Willon, "leaving me to pick up the bill. I'm going to have to learn to eat more quickly."

He stood up and walked across to the counter, pulling a wallet out of his pocket as he did so. Willon inspected the wine bottle; half full, still. He pushed the cork back in, slipped the bottle into his camera bag and joined Toulis as he finished paying.

Chapter 7

Toulis piloted his own flitter. It was an eight-seater model, but with the four back seats removed and the space used for carrying personal effects. He waited for Willon to fasten his cross harness and powered up the engine. He flicked on the communicator and set it to the standard Air Traffic Control frequency.

"Flitter to Air Traffic Control, I wish to leave."

"I hear you flitter." The voice was calm and matter-of-fact. Willon wondered if Gillik had put one of his own men in charge. He assumed so.

Then the voice came on again. "Towers have been warned, but personally, I'd go fast and low and downriver until you're out of range, in case the useless wazzocks forget what I've just told them." Willon nodded happily to himself; Yes, Gillik had put one of his own men in charge.

Toulis raised the flitter sedately until it was about ten feet above the ground.

"Are the towers tracking us?"

Willon looked round. "Yes."

The flitter leapt forward. Willon was first pushed back into his seat by the acceleration, and then was thrown sideways as Toulis turned the flitter sharply sideways and brought it down under the bow of a slow moving ferry. Toulis spun his craft quickly to avoid a small pleasure boat that had previously been hidden by the ferry. He turned to Willon. "Sorry, a middle-aged accountant doesn't often get the chance to play." Willon just shook his head, speechless, unable to take his eyes of the bowsprit of a yacht that seemed about to skewer him. Toulis rolled the flitter and went through the gap between the two yachts, Willon hanging helpless in his cross-harness. Screened by the river traffic, Toulis slowed the acceleration and headed downstream. After a couple of miles Toulis brought the flitter up in a slow climb.

"Air traffic control to flitter, come in please."

Toulis flicked the communicator to open.

"Flitter here, what can we do for you, Air Traffic Control?"

"Just to comment that it is lucky the ferry captain was wearing brown corduroy britches. Have a good trip flitter; Air Traffic Control, out."

Toulis engaged the cruise control and leaned back in his seat. He glanced at Willon.

"Wasn't that fun?" Before Willon had a chance to answer Toulis continued, "anyway, it's always good to keep in practice. Now then, I'm going to have to have a long chat to my office."

Half an hour later he came off his phone. He sighed.

"There's good news and bad news. Firstly, as I asked, they have been digging into LCS. They expected ownership to be vested in a number of shell companies, but actually it appears to be perfectly legitimate. It has shareholders, it's properly listed, and it even has prestigious directors. Haldar was right; apparently one of them is the governor's aunt, his stepmother's sister, Lucille Stilan. I've told them to dig deeper, but I'm not hopeful of finding anything else."

"Is that the good news or the bad news?"

"On the balance, it's bad. The good news is that some bright girl in the office thought to do a check on warehousing that we are insuring that is in any way linked to LCS. They found one property that is held in the name of Lucille Stilan. It may be that it is property she owns, but it is on the LCS policy."

"Worth checking out?"

"Yes, I think it calls for a quiet visit, ideally when no one is about. We'll go back to my office and I'll make arrangements. Anyway, Haldar told me to tell you the story of our exploits. So break out that half bottle of wine you've got hidden in your bag and I'll tell you a story."

*****

Toulis had his office in a block overlooking the Colitas-Tiffany canal, which marks the edge of both city and business district. He had a small apartment in the same block, and the flitter was garaged on the roof. Toulis led Willon into the kitchen-dining room of his apartment. Willon glanced round it. There was one window overlooking the canal and the gardens beyond, standard resin-cast furniture, usual facilities; but there was nothing too expensive, and few signs of personality. Toulis noticed his brief inspection.

"Yes, it's just a company apartment, I happen to be living here at the moment, but I wouldn't call it home. I've got a house in a fishing village along the coast, that's home." His tone was such as to discourage further questions.

After making coffee, Toulis switched on the holo-projector and loaded the map of the city. Scrolling through he pointed to a nondescript warehouse near the harbour, set back a little from the Colitas wharf.

"That's the one. You can see that it is larger than the one at Kenehan. I'd say that the storage space is equivalent to two storeys and there are offices or smaller store rooms on top of that." Toulis rotated the holo and pointed again. "Yes, you can see on this side, the top floor was added some time after the warehouse was built, it doesn't cover the entire warehouse, and there is a landing pad taking up perhaps a third of the warehouse roof."

They both studied the holo for some minutes before Toulis spoke,

"I think we ought to go in from above. There are only two doors in at the ground floor, and entering that way will be far too obvious." He zoomed out to try and see various ways of approaching the building. "The problem is there is no way to be inconspicuous in the flitter, and climbing the walls is probably out."

"What about a floater?" asked Willon. Toulis appeared bemused, so Willon explained. "Channel Six does the traffic reports and we have a couple of floaters for the presenters, so they can drift quietly along at pretty much any altitude to do the traffic reports. We also use them to get good camera angles."

"Can you get us one?"

"No problem; I occasionally do the traffic reports and the garage knows me, so they'll not have a problem with me just collecting one."

"Right, I'll fix us a meal and we wait for dark."

*****

Haldar stood in the airlock of the Suborbital. The crewman with him pressed the button to cycle the air out and Haldar checked the tell-tales on the display projected onto his helmet visor. That done, he ran through the manual checks, tapping the gloved fingers of his left hand on the back of his right hand as a way of ticking them off. He smiled to see the crewman do the same. Eventually his companion turned to face him and gave him a 'thumbs up'. Haldar returned the gesture and the crewman turned and opened the outside door of the airlock. There, filling their field of view was the Taurus, matching them, vector for vector. Haldar watched the great warship with affection. The great red bull painted on the bow had obviously been re-painted recently, the rest of the hull was painted black, a score of subtly different shades as generations of junior ratings had been despatched outside to repaint a section. A score of domes and turrets were visible, the weaponry 'run out' and prepared for action. He was irresistibly reminded of a guard dog his family had had when he was a child. It had seen off an intruder and walked with a swagger of hours after, baring its teeth at the slightest hint of a threat. The old Taurus was swaggering, her teeth bared and her flanks dimly shining in the starlight. Behind her, as if arranged for her benefit, lay the rest of the galaxy, a thick belt of stars, brighter in comparison with the relative emptiness above and below. Even after all these years, Haldar felt his eyes prickle slightly with tears.

The crewman swung a line thrower away from the wall and started to cock it. The line thrower was a windlass crossbow, and there was enough energy in the cocked bow to throw a line as far as was needed at this sort of altitude. The crewman checked to see that the line was running free and that Haldar was not in the way and, taking careful aim, fired. The line-carrying bolt flew towards the Taurus and the magnetic bolt hit three feet from the opening airlock, forward of the main armament.

"Good shooting," Haldar said, and meant it, even if the crewman couldn't hear him. A sloppy shot would have left him with a long walk in magnetic boots before he got to the airlock. Haldar clipped his suit harness to the wire. The crewman checked the clip and tapped him on the shoulder. Haldar stepped forward onto the non-ferrous panel and then launched himself out along the line. His initial thrust was nearly enough; he only had to pull himself hand over hand for the last few yards. Finally he allowed himself to drop down towards the airlock. With his feet firmly clamped to the landing panel, he unclipped his suit harness from the line and onto the ship, then reached out and slapped the magnetic bolt. It switched off and the line fell away to be reeled in by the crewman. The panel Haldar was standing on retracted into the airlock and the doors closed behind him. He checked the tell-tales on his suit and when they eventually stabilised on full atmosphere he carefully opened his helmet. Assured that all was well, he took off his suit and hung it carefully in the locker provided. The locker still bore the crest of the Salid Empire, and had only recently been repainted in the proper colours. He glanced round the airlock. Away from the walls, the floor was polished by the tread of innumerable boots. Still, the seals looked new. If the airlock was anything to go by, old Taurus was still a well-run ship. With this private observation, he opened the inner door to enter the ship proper.

He was met by Captain Aldor Issil. The gravity of his office had never weighed heavily on Aldor. When he was an ensign he had been described as showing the dignity and affection of a wet dog. Now, he restricted his greetings to a warm handshake, but more formal captains normally greeted visitors at the bridge rather than the airlock.

"Haldar, good to see you welcome aboard."

Haldar warmly returned the handshake. He had served with Aldor on the Taurus as an ensign.

"How's the old rust bucket doing?"

Aldor's grin grew wider. "We're thinking of having a party; someone has been through the logs and has discovered that she's coming up to a thousand years old."

Haldar's look of surprise was real. "We all knew she was a fair age, but no one realised she was that old."

Aldor slapped Haldar on the back and led him to the bridge. "We've got the records out so everyone can see them. We knew she was built as a system defence boat, but we're not sure where. She was brought into our system with a heavy tug, and of course once the tug left she was stuck here until someone brought another tug to collect her. They didn't have one big enough in the last centuries of the Empire. So here she stayed."

Haldar tried to get a word in "and she's still in full working order?"

"Absolutely, you know we have been reverse engineering most of the parts? We heard about some old Imperial stocks tucked away the other side of the sector, sent a tech to check, and he came back with several tons of useful bits, but more importantly, a lot of engineering drawings as well. We've even got the chronometer in the captain's cabin working, first time for over a century."

Faced with a tidal wave of enthusiasm, which in all candour Haldar had to admit that he shared, he decided to just go with the flow. He was introduced to the officers, some of whom he knew, if only vaguely. He was wined and dined in the officers' mess where the toast was to the health of an emperor two centuries dead; he was asked to head-up the tour of inspection and carefully avoided embarrassing people by finding anything wrong. That being said, there wasn't much to find. Indeed, at one point he wondered whether Aldor hadn't achieved a military first; commanding a vessel which was both capable of combat and could pass inspection.

Eventually, as he shared a late night drink in the captain's cabin, he brought the conversation round to the shooting down of the Starmancer. Early in the evening toasts had been drunk to the old ship's success, but now Haldar gently tried to probe more deeply.

"So Aldor, exactly how did you arrive over the Starmancer barely half an hour after they attacked?"

It was well known throughout the navy that Aldor couldn't lie. He reputedly grew noticeably embarrassed just exaggerating. In this case, he was silent for some time and then replied,

"it is something I wondered about, as well. About a month ago, we got our orders for this tour. It was suggested that at some time we did some atmosphere work, and I did think I'd take her into the gas giant."

This Haldar could understand. During wartime, system defence boats like the Taurus would lurk in the atmosphere of a gas giant. There, they were undetectable, and could also quietly refuel from the atmosphere. Then, if hostile forces did enter the system, the boats would suddenly sally out, wreaking havoc among an unsuspecting enemy before retiring once more to their lair. Any system defence boat captain worth his salt would make sure his crews were used to working in that sort of atmosphere.

"But then," Aldor continued, "we got a message that we were being diverted to Tsarina. Silly thing really; but an old commander of the Taurus, Tarl Horvin, was ill and not expected to live much longer. He had expressed a wish to see his old ship again. Anyway, the request came via the Governor's private office, and so we talked with them, and it was agreed that I'd bring the old ship in at a thousand feet over his country estate, and his family would wheel his bed out so he could see us. We made a couple of passes and got a message from his daughter saying how grateful old Tarl was, and as we were moving away, we got an alarm call saying that an unidentified ship had entered atmosphere and was coming in fast; as we were the closest, we were sent to investigate. As we got closer, we got the holo footage, so we knew what was going on and could go in ready to strike."

Haldar looked at his old colleague's face. He knew that from Aldor's point of view this tale was absolutely true. It was the sort of thing Aldor would do. When he'd commanded one of the navy's patrol craft, he'd detoured half way across the system and brought the ship down between two private cars on a hospital vehicle park so a crewman could be there when his wife gave birth to their first child. Haldar remembered the incident with affection. He'd won a hundred Thalian Credits off one of the local magistrates who hadn't believed that the Governor would grant Aldor a full pardon. It struck Haldar that someone out there had known Aldor and had played him perfectly. The problem is, pretty well everyone in both navy and marines knew Aldor, so that didn't really help.

Aldor continued. "But I did wonder about it. I even checked—Tarl *was* ill, he was delighted, but he hadn't asked. His daughter says she didn't ask, but that an old comrade of his dropped by and suggested it."

"Who was the old comrade? Do I know him?"

"You will do," Aldor replied with confidence. "It was Doran Stilan."

Haldar decided to try a bit more probing.

"So you think Doran Stilan knew the Starmancers were going to strike?"

"Yes." Aldor was definite. "After all, he does lead the Watch Company, so I assumed Intelligence had got word that something might be happening and brought us in, with Tarl as an excuse."

"So nothing else was said?"

Aldor smiled. "Nothing, which is why I rather assumed that it was Intelligence."

"That seems to sort my little problem out. Watch Company don't speak to mere mortals like me."

Aldor frowned. "I know that there is no love lost between the Watch Company and the Navy, but I hadn't heard there was bad blood between them and the Governor's Investigation Office."

Haldar nodded; Aldor, he trusted, and the man deserved to know the truth. Indeed as captain of the Taurus, he needed to know the truth. "Watch Company report to Doran Stilan and he reports to the Governor in person. They don't work through normal Intelligence channels. Because they're Uncle Doran's private army, this means they're effectively unaccountable and out-of-control. They've got their fingers in too many pies." He shrugged. "Ah well, any chance of me borrowing your gig to get home? Captain Gillik will not be happy if I try to borrow his suborbital twice in the same day."

"Possessive, is he?"

"Remember when you first wanted to borrow your father's flitter? Gillik didn't actually lecture me on unsuitable girls or the dangers of drink, but it came awfully close."

Aldor walked across to his desk and switched on the communicator. "Captain here, can I have my gig ready to take a guest down to," he stopped speaking and glanced at Haldar, "Kaunas City, please." Haldar nodded his agreement.

Aldor switched off the communicator. "They'll be ten minutes; I'll show you the way."

*****

After they had eaten, Toulis changed into a pair of nondescript working overalls and produced another set for Willon. Then he produced a bag from where it was hidden behind a cupboard, full of canned and dried foods.

"Have you had any weapons training?" he asked.

"Well, I'm a member of my district militia company," Willon answered.

"I'll take that as a 'no' then."

From the bag Toulis produced two handguns. "They're ceramic, with no metal parts, use caseless ammunition and have a built-in silencer."

Willon took one and examined it carefully. "Why not just use a conventional energy pistol?"

"Energy pistols show up on energy scanners."

Toulis ran through the safety catch, magazine-eject and reload routines, and Willon carefully put the weapon in the side pocket of the overalls.

"I hope we don't need them," Toulis said as they left, "but too many potential witnesses have been dying recently."

Willon led the way to the Tsarina Broadcasting building along the upper walkways. Below them ground cars and heavy delivery vehicles thundered, above them were the flitters and light air traffic. Willon led them off the moving walkway, took a lift up two levels and eventually came to a door marked Channel Six Support.

"You'll have to stick with me. The exit for the floaters is out the back, and there is no pedestrian access there."

"I suppose I can try and behave like a journalist," Toulis replied.

"Don't bother, I'm going to try and pass you off as an auditor from central funding who wants to know why we have floaters."

Willon opened the door and entered. He waved casually to people who were working at benches strewn with a miscellany of electrical and mechanical parts.

"Don't worry people, I'm just here for a floater, I've got to take an auditor out, he wants to see why we need them."

"There were cat calls from various more distant benches, but a tall man making himself a drink in the kitchen area put his mug down and came across.

"Hi Willon, take Number Two. I want to check out Number One—apparently it drifts left when you leave it in neutral."

"Thanks Hal." Willon went across to the board and took the keys. He glanced back at Toulis. "This way sir, let's leave these busy people to get on with it."

Toulis followed him silently. Willon led the way down a short corridor and unlocked the door at the end. In the middle of the floor sat something which might have passed for a kitchen table that had been laid upside down on the floor with its legs sticking up into the air. Willon stepped onto the middle of the floater and motioned for Toulis to follow him. Then Willon tapped one of the legs and a safety rail was activated, joining all four legs together.

Willon said, conversationally, "safety feature. If we're too heavy, nothing happens. Once the rail is in place, the exit door will open."

As if on cue, a large double door started to slide to one side, leaving them overlooking the city. At the same time, something Toulis mentally pigeon-holed as a fifth leg, came up from the middle of the floater. Willon clasped it and manually extended a joystick.

"Simple joystick controls, pull back for up, push forward for down, left or right to turn."

"What about acceleration?"

"What acceleration? You get three levels of speed, loitering, very slow and slow. You flick this switch here to shift between speeds."

Willon flicked the switch and pulled back the joystick a little. The floater rose off the floor and moved sedately through the door and out into the cool night air. Willon flicked the switch again and the floater accelerated briefly. At a genteel twenty miles an hour they glided silently through the night. Abandoning the controls, Willon knelt down and opened a hatch in the floor.

"There are half a dozen storage bins built into the floor. Most contain recording and broadcasting gear, but these could be useful." He passed a pair of goggles to Toulis. "Night-vision goggles, and pretty good ones at that."

Toulis put them on and stared around him. "You're right, they are pretty good. Standard military issue, I'd guess."

"Probably; I think we scrounged them from the marines when we were doing a documentary about military training."

*****

The floater made reasonable progress, but Toulis seemed dissatisfied. Willon watched him out of the corner of his eye and waited for him to say something. Finally, Toulis said "a little conspicuous, aren't we?"

Willon managed to look surprised. "What do you mean?"

Toulis gestured around him, "I've seen capital ships with fewer navigation lights."

"Ah," Willon said. "I thought you meant the broadcast screen."

"What broadcast screen?"

Willon pointed downwards, "All round the sides of the base there's a continuous scrolling news feed." He produced a headset from one of the stowage boxes and stood up. "Don't worry; we're going to be so conspicuous that no one will look at us."

Plugging the headset into the fifth leg, he pressed the call button.

A female voice answered. "Tsarina Broadcasting, Channel Six, switchboard."

"Hi Deleen," Willon said, "can you patch me through to Mord, please?"

"Hi Willon, will do."

There were thirty seconds of discordant music before a male voice cut in.

"Hi, Mord here."

Willon answered. "Hi Mord, Willon here. I'm out on a floater on a jolly, and it'd be useful if I could at least show some footage to cover my back."

There was a laugh at the other end and then Mord said, "you've got the usual camera array?"

"Yes."

"Then we'll fit in some Kaunas City by night footage. Swing in and out of the walkways, we can have you shoot and broadcast live. It'll save having to pad out the show with archive stuff. Some of that has been so regenerated that I'd swear we're creating an alternate reality."

"Thanks Mord, I'll switch the array on and you cut across and introduce us and work us into show." Willon thought briefly, "I'll run the bad music gag as well."

Mord laughed, "go for it."

Willon turned to Toulis. "There you are; anyone who sees us and wonders what we're doing can just switch to Channel Six and see through our cameras.

Channel Six is quite popular anyway, a creative combination of news, bad music and inane chat."

Toulis shrugged. "Well, it's novel."

Willon grinned. "You squat down there and act like a technician. When we come to the building we'll over-fly it a time or two and you can decide how we get in."

Willon headed towards the warehouse. All the while he was listening to the program in his headset. Finally he heard Mord introduce him. He ignored it and let Mord try a second time before he spoke.

"Sorry Mord, had the sound turned off to block out that *'Seyman and the Jiggettes'* rubbish you've been playing all week. It's a beautiful, peaceful night here over by the Colitas-Tiffany canal, and I didn't want to spoil the atmosphere."

Toulis peered over the edge of the floater. They were approaching the warehouse now. Ignoring Willon, who was burbling away in a cheerfully meaningless fashion, he concentrated on the job in hand. There were three flitters on the warehouse roof, accessible from the offices. Toulis adjusted his night-vision goggles to try and get better magnification and contrast. The flitters were armed; he recognized the rocket pods folded into the utility area. If they had rockets then there would be other stuff as well. He tugged at Willon's leg, and without changing his tone Willon glanced down at him. Toulis made a circling gesture. Willon nodded and, still talking glibly about the courting couples walking hand in hand along the canal-side footpath, he brought the floater round in a long slow turn. Toulis could see that there were people watching them from the warehouse roof. He tugged at Willon's leg again and gestured. Willon saw the men and swung his camera array across to cover the warehouse.

"And it isn't just romance by starlight here," be burbled. "There are still folk having to work this evening; a big hello to the security staff at the warehouse here! Any requests? Just send them in, and Mord at Midnight on good old Channel Six will play them for you." Willon stopped briefly before adding, "and it's back to Mord for another classic from that sultry chanteuse, *Dwine Tillanvor.*" Willon glanced at his screen before adding, "and she's singing the song she made famous, 'Dreams of Ancient Earth.' I'm going to stay on the line and listen to that one myself."

Willon switched off the mike and glanced across to the empty roof. "That cleared it faster than an air strike."

"Can you replay the footage of those guys, please?" Toulis asked.

"Sure. There's a screen tucked in stowage. Pull it out, and I just have to hook it into the control here."

Toulis opened the lid and found the screen. By now they were passing over the warehouse and he felt particularly exposed. Willon plugged the screen in and played back the last few minutes' footage. Toulis halted the footage and zoomed in.

"Yes, I thought so; look at those shoulder flashes. 'Watch Company'."

Willon glanced at the screen. "Aren't they the ones who broke up the disturbances at the Space Port last year?"

"Yes, a brawl between a freighter crew and a shore patrol from Taurus got out of hand; the Watch Company went in and left five people dead, four of them from the Taurus." Toulis switched off the screen and lowered it back out of the way. "The Watch Company aren't exactly known for their courtesy or even-handedness."

"Isn't this getting awfully political?" Willon asked.

"If it is, it's because politicians are prone to good old-fashioned corruption and graft. A lot of elite forces are more like well-trained thugs forming the bodyguard for a politician who's just a gangster with social aspirations." Toulis peered over the edge again. "Fetch us round over the roof again, but drop six foot as you do it. I want a course which will pass over the roof every ten minutes."

Willon swung the floater round in a long loop bringing it slightly lower as he did so. As they passed over the roof for a second time, Toulis looked up at him. "See you here in ten minutes."

Toulis dropped over the side of the floater and landed on a flitter. He scrambled over the side and dropped to the floor. On hands and knees, he crawled across the roof and came to a skylight. He peered through the glass; there was some light down there, at least enough to show him that the warehouse was stacked with packing cases. He searched in the shadow at the side of the skylight, found the catch and pushed it. Then he gently opened the skylight. Below him, he could see no one, and opening the skylight had produced no response. Swiftly he produced a spool of fine cord from the pocket of his overalls and clipped it to his belt. He fastened the end around the catch and lowered himself down, hand over hand.

He landed softly on the top packing case and glanced round. The cases were stacked high, the top ones no more than eight feet from the roof. Still, there was no one about, so he drew his handgun from the pocket in his overalls and laid it on the packing case next to him. Then he took a small pry bar from out of another pocket and started to open the lid of the next packing case along. He winced as the wood tore with a cracking sound. Somewhere below him he could hear feet. He risked a glance into the now open packing case. All he could see was an exquisitely carved chair back. He crouched low on his perch and waited in silence.

"Gregor, you there?" A voice came up from below him.

"Over here." This second voice was from over to his left.

"What were that noise?"

"Dunno."

"It could be on the crates. I'll get the lift."

There was the sound of footsteps, then muffled comments and finally the loud hum of a repulsion motor.

Toulis lay flat, but he realised that up here he was totally devoid of cover. He tried to fix the position of the lift by the sound of its motor. He turned and aimed his handgun in that direction. The humming was getting louder and suddenly he saw a helmet. He carefully pointed his weapon at it, as more and more of the helmet became visible.

"There's something there!"

Toulis fired and the speaker dropped, but Toulis didn't think he'd hit him. In all candour, he was forced to admit to himself that he rarely hit anything.

"You found the bastard," yelled the second voice.

Toulis needed time; any moment now they'd just call for back-up. He fired another shot to try and keep their heads down. He cursed himself as an idiot. He was an insurance loss adjuster; his back-up was a journalist, for gods' sake. Toulis reminded himself that he had spent his ten years on warships as a general engineer, not a marine, and that was twenty years ago. He lay still and listened. He suspected his opponents were doing the same. He started groping for the pry bar and asked himself when he was going to start acting his age and employ professionals to do this sort of stuff. He found the pry bar, grasped it and threw it as far as possible. He heard it clatter across some packing cases and then the clang as it hit the floor. This was followed by the hum of the repulsion motor moving in that direction.

Frantically, he thrust his handgun back into his pocket and scrambled up the line, at any moment expecting to hear shouts or weapons fire. At the top, he pulled himself over the edge of the skylight and lay flat on the roof. He risked a glance around. He could see the floater coming back for him, the scrolling text around the base telling the world that at the moment Channel Six was featuring 'Mord at Midnight; Nobody does it better'. Toulis shut the skylight, wound in the cord and put the spool back in his pocket. The floater was almost upon him. He crouched and then, as the floater passed, jumped onto the flitter from where he was able to grab the floater. Willon reached down and helped pull him up.

Suddenly the door on the roof burst open and figures rushed out toward the flitters.

Toulis threw himself flat on the deck and drew his handgun.

"This is about to end badly."

Willon said, "it'll be in front of witnesses" and pressed the button on his mike.

"Hi Mord, just to tell you that we've had someone pass us a request up here."

Mord's voice came over the system. "You see viewers, so important are your requests our skilled staff will break into the show half way through one of my stories just to get them to us." There was a pause for a sound effect raspberry then Mord's voice was back. "So what is the request, Willon?"

"It was just they wanted us to stop you telling your story, Mord."

Behind them, the figures were climbing into the flitters and taking off, ignoring the floater. Toulis watched them, mystified.

"I'd love to know what's happening."

At that point his phone rang.

*****

Taran was rapidly losing faith in the flitter he had stolen. His plan had been to keep at treetop height, not go too fast, and weave his way through so that the taller trees were between him and possible observation.

This failed because the brute had too high a stalling speed; he was forced to fly faster and higher than he wanted. At one point some woodland creature had defecated on him, so he flew higher still. After a couple of miles he spotted a road going in the right direction and dropped down to follow that. Five minutes later, cursing, he was forced up again when a heavy logging float came round a bend in the middle of the road. Then he realised that the road was taking him inexorably closer to the river, with its heavy traffic. Finally, just to prove that it wasn't going to be his day, it started to rain. He closed the canopy and decided to give up on subtlety and just kept the machine high enough to avoid all the trees. He headed the machine directly towards where he hoped Kaunas City was. It had the space port and even if the local planetary contact couldn't help, he hoped he would be able to get a berth off-planet as a working crewman.

This plan seemed good to him, and he was feeling quietly confident as he flew the craft east. It was at this point the engine started cutting out. Hastily, Taran searched for an open space to land, and managed to get the flitter almost down when the engine cut out entirely and the machine dropped the last six feet.

He checked the various dials on the panel in front of him. Fuel full, temperature normal, altitude zero, and various mechanical and electrical functions all seemed to be fine. He cursed and switched the electronics off to save power. All the dials went to zero, except the fuel. He cursed again and switched the electronics back on. All the dials registered, except for the fuel which this time slowly settled down to zero. He switched the electronics off again and waited, but the fuel dial didn't budge. He cursed for a third time and, by now unwilling to trust the flitter's systems, he went to the back and manually checked the fuel cells. Empty, all six of them.

He looked around. He was in a clearing in the woods that was perhaps half a mile across at the longest point. The trees seemed strange to him, some were squat and bulbous, some were elongated and bent into strange shapes, their branches curved and bent at strange angles. The ground was covered with something which he labelled grass, but might not have been. He opened the door and stepped out, and sank up to his ankles in the soft ground. Out of the ground burst quite a number of some sort of crab, but with ten legs and pincers at both ends. They hissed and clicked their pincers at him but then moved away and disappeared back into the soft ground. Taran hastily climbed back into the flitter. Fortunately the vehicle's weight was well distributed; it seemed to be stable. He sat back down in his seat and fumbled for his utility belt. He pulled out a ration bar and peeled off the plastic covering. One thing he'd learned during his time as a mercenary and pirate, if nothing is happening, eat and sleep. As the rain beat down on the flitter canopy he chewed the bar, and it was still raining when he fell asleep.

He woke up with a start some hours later. It was dark. He'd slept longer than he'd intended. He stared at the two local contact numbers on his head-up display. His options appeared restricted to walking to Kaunas City or calling the numbers. The first he instinctively dismissed. He was a starship crewman; if a spaceport bar was more than a mile away, he'd look for transport. So which number?

After some thought, he decided on the new one, but wasn't happy. So far he wasn't particularly impressed with the new patron. However, orders overcame his distrust. He dialled the number and waited. An automated system answered, informed him that his call and position were logged and switched off.

Taran felt out of his depth here. He'd never had to use a local contact before, but comrades who had over the years had told tales of being hidden by beautiful women and smuggled out wrapped in carpet. None of them had mentioned automated systems.

He looked at the first number. Their normal patron had a good reputation. Somewhat indecisively, he dialled that number, too.

*****

Toulis glanced at his phone. "It's the other number."

Willon glance back at him over his shoulder. "What other number?"

"I'm the local contact for Wayland Strang and his organisation."

The phone continued to ring. "Well, you'd better answer it, then."

Toulis pressed the button. "Yes?"

The voice at the other end was hesitant. "I'm Taran, I'm trying to get the local contact." He remembered himself. "Sorry yes, acting corporal, Assault team, three years seniority on current ship."

"What ship?"

"Falling Angel"

"Where are you? I'll have to arrange pick up."

Taran was hesitant. "The other number said they'd got a lock on my phone."

"What other number?"

Slowly Toulis managed to get the story out of Taran. Willon listened in. By now he'd got the floater back to the bay at Support. Toulis was still talking.

"You'll have to leave the flitter and take cover."

"But it's raining here." The voice was a little petulant.

"Taran, we just saw three Special Forces flitters take off on alert and they might be heading for you. Get out of that bluidy flitter."

There was grumbled assent at the far end.

Toulis continued, "I am going to try and get a pick up, but it might be military. The person who contacts you will ask for Taran of the Falling Angel. Got that?"

Again, there was grumbled assent, but this time Toulis thought he could hear boots squelching through mud. He cut the connection and immediately dialled a different number.

"Haldar here."

"Toulis here; where are you?"

"I'm in the Captain's gig, coming down from the Taurus."

"That's handy; I've got a job for you."

*****

Haldar switched his phone off and turned to the Lieutenant commanding the Captain's gig.

"Do you mind if we put in a diversion? I've been asked to collect someone."

The lieutenant looked up from the controls. "Not at all, sir, where are they?"

Haldar gave him the coordinates. The Lieutenant looked surprised.

"Yes lieutenant, I know. Not all that far from the site of the Starmancer attack. This is because the gentleman in question is a Starmancer and a survivor of the action."

The lieutenant passed the coordinates to the helmsman.

"Will there be any … difficulties sir?" The lieutenant's tone indicated that he didn't mind if there were. While his vessel was called the Captain's gig, only the low power of the drives stopped it being classed as the second most powerful warship in the Tsarina system. The Taurus and her gig had been designed to standards and specifications laid down in a more dangerous universe.

"There might be, I suspect that someone else wants to get him first and we have to stop them. With force if needed."

"Who should we expect?"

Haldar tried to keep his voice noncommittal; "Three armed flitters, manned by 'Watch Company' personnel, perhaps."

The Lieutenant pressed a button on his desk and the action station siren sounded throughout the small ship. He waited two minutes and switched it off. "That should have given them long enough." He grinned at Haldar and then spoke into the microphone, his voice echoing round the ship on the speakers. "We're going in to pick someone up. There might be hostile action taken against us. Keep an eye open for armed flitters." Then he added. "The Captain would not be happy if his gig got scratched, so keep alert."

He turned back to Haldar. "We'll be on our way."

*****

As they came down above the clearing Haldar could easily see the abandoned flitter. There was no one near it; Haldar assumed that the Starmancer was watching them from cover.

"I will take us down sir, but gently." The Lieutenant was at his shoulder, also perusing the screen. "I thought we could lower a ladder rather than land, I'd rather have altitude and visibility if possible."

Haldar looked up from the screen. "Carry on Lieutenant, I'll go to the hatch and prepare to land."

He made his way aft to the lower hatch. The turret gunner saw him, nodded politely and went back to watching the skies and his instruments.

Haldar unclipped the hatch and one of the two marines whose action station this was, assisted him in opening it. They swung the winch over and started to lower the ladder. Haldar stepped onto it and allowed it to carry him down. After the controlled environment of the gig the air was cool and damp. He could smell the dampness of the forest. The ship halted at above treetop height, allowing Haldar a good view of the flora and fauna of the upper canopy. Strange smelling blossoms dangled in long strings from the upper branches. A small kyout stopped to watch him, a squirming bird grasped in a seven clawed hand. It chattered furiously at him, thrusting engorged heliotrope coloured genitals at him as a warning gesture.

As the ladder lowered, Haldar looked round, and thought he could see a figure watching him from behind a tree. As the ladder touched the ground, Haldar stepped away from the ladder and turned towards the half-seen figure.

Haldar shouted. "I'm here to collect Taran of the Falling Angel"

The figure behind the tree moved indecisively away from the tree, but didn't step into the open.

Haldar shouted again, "I'm here to collect Taran of the Falling Angel." He waited briefly. "Make your mind up, there could be others on the way and they're not your friends."

The incongruously dressed figure, in business suit, body armour and helmet, made its way towards him. Haldar stepped forward to meet the Starmancer and held out a hand.

"I'm Haldar, Toulis asked me to collect you for him."

The Starmancer switched his carbine from right hand to left and then hastily wiped his right hand on his trousers before shaking hands with Haldar.

"I'm Taran."

Above them was a sharp crack, the noise you get when you fire a heavy laser in dense atmosphere. Haldar glanced upwards, the turret traversed and fired again.

"Grab the ladder, let's get out of here."

Haldar stepped onto the ladder and grabbed it firmly with both hands. Hesitating briefly, Taran slung his carbine over his shoulder and also got hold of the ladder, which immediately started to rise.

The gig was also rising, they were now above treetop height and Haldar heard the crack of the turret laser again. This time he could see the target, an incoming missile which flashed into incandescence as the laser beam hit it. Then Haldar heard the forward turret open fire. He turned on the ladder, trying to see what it was firing at in time to see a burning flitter crash into the trees.

"Let's get up this ladder."

Behind and below them there was an explosion as the flitter's fuel cells exploded, Haldar felt the blast as a wave of warm air swept over him and his nostrils and eyes stung with the smell of partially burnt fuel.

The Starmancer, perhaps more used to this sort of situation, needed no encouragement and climbed up the ladder ahead of him. At the hatch they were met by the two marines, one of whom courteously relieved Taran of the carbine, the other took his pistol and boot knife. Taran appeared lost and one of the marines reassured him, "We'll put these in the arms locker, they'll be safe there."

The aft turret gunner traversed rapidly and fired. Out there, past the gunner, Haldar saw a flash; something had been hit, but he couldn't see what. The rest of the ladder was now in, and Haldar and the other marine shut the hatch. Immediately the gig accelerated, climbing as she did. Haldar put his arm in a companionable way around Taran's shoulders. "You and I are going to have to have a little chat before this ship gets to the starport outside Kaunas City."

*****

As the gig neared the starport, Haldar was flicking though his notes. Taran was sitting at a table, chatting to the two marines and tucking into a Tsarina Navy ration pack with enthusiasm. Haldar had known easier interrogation suspects, but not many. Even on civilised planets, captured Starmancers could expect to be burned at the stake as a warning to others, so Taran had been almost pathetically grateful for reasonable treatment. Added to that, the destruction of the Falling Angel meant he didn't feel he was betraying anyone.

One of the marines came across to him. "Landing in five minutes sir, please strap in."

Haldar looked at the marine. "Strap in?" He allowed the surprise to register in his voice.

"Yes sir," the marine sounded a little apologetic, "It's a commercial spaceport so we tend to obey the regulations."

Haldar sighed ruefully. "Oh, so I'm not just going down on the ladder then."

The marine grinned openly. "Not if the Lieutenant might hear about it, sir."

Haldar made his way along to the bridge and strapped into a seat near the Lieutenant. "When we land I have to meet someone. I'd be grateful if you could hang around for a few minutes."

"Don't worry sir; for the officer who let us take on the Watch Company, we'll not even keep the meter running."

Haldar checked his notes again, and made a few written comments in the margins. The gig landed with the proper formality expected of her, and once the prescribed procedures had been followed the Lieutenant announced that he was lowering the ramp. Taking Taran with him, Haldar tramped down the ramp onto the hard standing. Walking across from the terminal building, he could see Toulis and Willon. He gestured to Taran to halt and they waited for the other two. On arrival Haldar made introductions.

Toulis turned and ostentatiously surveyed the area around them. "Well, your current office is difficult to bug; any obvious reason for meeting here?"

"This isn't an easy case," Haldar explained. "I've heard your tale over the phone. I can start things moving, but senior people are going to be very upset."

Willon looked nervous. "Should I leave at this point?"

Haldar shook his head. "You know enough to work it out for yourself." He gestured toward Taran. "Our friend here doesn't know a lot, but he knew it was a new patron. Word had leaked out that the new patron had enough influence to ensure that they wouldn't be bothered by patrol ships or inopportune military patrols."

Toulis spoke quietly. "And who have you fingered as the new patron?"

"It isn't easy to pinpoint one person," Haldar said. "Not with genuine evidence. The Watch Company is tainted. Their flitters attacked the gig, which seems like an act of desperation. I've had our technical people check out the new Local Contact number Taran had, and it led, through some interesting technical cut-outs, to the Watch Company HQ."

"And everyone knows that the Watch Company reports to Doran Stilan." Toulis allowed no emotion into his voice.

"He is their commanding officer, indeed their founder. I remember the presentation he made; he showed that it was important to have a quick reaction force outside the usual military structures and with loyalty solely to the Governor." Haldar too was careful to keep his voice expressionless. "He was allowed to have it, partially because I think it was felt it might keep him busy, give him something to do."

"And the furniture?"

"Funny you should mention it. The police raided the building –" here Haldar peered at his watch, "sorry, are *currently* raiding the building, as a result of an anonymous tip-off."

Toulis smiled. "Trans-world (Tsarina) Insurance will of course be grateful for the prompt action of the authorities."

"I also had a word with Aled, the Colonel of the Marines. I think he's a little put out over being caught flat footed over your mercenary invasion of the Border Kingdoms. The Marines have now moved with extreme prejudice against those Watch Company left alive. Most managed to surrender ... Ah sorry, forgetting myself." Haldar sketched a mock half-bow. "And the authorities have now disarmed the surviving members of the Watch Company. The unit will be disbanded; the official line will be that corruption was discovered in lower ranks."

Willon asked, "and in reality?"

"However much the politicians howl, the Watch Company no longer exists; those who survived arrest will be questioned. Those who come clean quickly might well stay in the services, but spread among other military units. Almost certainly not the navy, though, unless they seriously upset the staff doing the assigning. Those who know what was really going on will be held for trial. Probably on the Taurus where I can guarantee that they'll live long enough to give evidence."

"What about Doran Stilan?" Willon asked.

"You and I are going to have a meeting with the Governor. As we all know, it's political. You and I have to make sure he does the right thing." Haldar turned to Taran, who was gazing at two young women walking across the hard standing to a neighbouring ship.

"Taran, I'm sending you up in the gig to the Taurus. The captain is a decent enough bloke. He will hide you. If you hang around down here, someone will ask questions, and even perfectly respectable people will want you dead."

Taran nodded. Haldar wasn't sure whether the Starmancer appeared relieved or not. Then Taran asked, "what about my ship credit?"

"Sorry?"

"You know, my ship credit. I had over six thousand Thalian Credits banked with them."

Haldar seemed to be bemused. "But the ship was destroyed."

Toulis interrupted. "Ship credit isn't stored on ship. The vast majority of the money will actually be banked somewhere. The patron might know where."

Haldar then turned to Toulis.

"And I suspect you'd better leave as well. There are going to be unanswered questions and people might try and fling mud around in their defence."

"I've got people to see as well as sorting out Taran's ship credit," Toulis answered, "so I'll just take the next ship out."

"Don't be in too big a hurry. Keep in touch; I might have news for you, hopefully in the next twelve hours."

Haldar held out his hand and Toulis shook it, then Toulis shook hands with Willon, and turned and walked back to the terminal.

Haldar turned to Taran. "Best of luck."

Taran hesitated, and then saluted. He turned and walked back up the ramp into the gig.

"And now we need to see the Governor. I'll phone for an official ground car, it's so much easier to get into the palace in one of them."

*****

Willon had been in the Palace before. It was not merely a residence, it was also an administrative complex and barracks. The gardens, at least, were open to the citizens of Kaunas City.

The ground car made somewhat stately progress through checkpoints and guard posts before coming to a halt in an inner garage. Haldar led Willon down a corridor, stopping at the lift. He waved his pass across a scanner and the lift door opened. They were immediately checked by two marine guards manning the lift and, on Haldar being recognized, were taken up four floors. There they were let out into a waiting room where Haldar introduced himself to the receptionist.

Directed to a row of empty chairs, they were left to their own devices while the receptionist passed on their request for an interview. Willon knew that it could take any of the broadcasters two or three days to get an interview, but suspected the military could do it faster. Still, he was surprised when ten minutes later the receptionist told them to go through.

Willon had met the Governor, Vladimir Kaunas, before. He'd even conducted a short interview with him at a flower and produce show, so he wasn't thrown by the man's informality.

When they were shown in, the Governor was standing at an easel, and was attempting to paint the scene from his office window. He put down his brush and turned to face them.

"So Haldar, what have you found?" Before Haldar could answer, Vladimir added, "I have already had to sign the documentation dealing with the Watch Company."

"Well, the rest of the military will be happy that particular private army is being wound up."

The Governor sat on the edge of the desk. "So how far does it go?"

"All the way to the top; Doran Stilan is in it up to his neck, as is his wife. At the very least it's a spectacular insurance fraud. At the very least we have a ship-load of dead Starmancers and a fair number of LCS employees have died in unexplained circumstances. To this you can add the Border Kingdoms debacle, Abate, a lot of dead women who were in the facility when it was destroyed and an undeclared war on Wayland Strang."

"So good old uncle Doran couldn't resist making a bit of money on the side?"

Haldar nodded his agreement.

"Evidence?"

Haldar glanced at Willon. "What do you think of the case? Would your editor let you run the story?"

Willon was taken by surprise. He'd not expected this question. Then he answered carefully. "I think so. I think he'd reckon that it was worth putting out there on the grounds that Doran Stilan wouldn't risk suing us, as he might lose in the courts."

Haldar turned back to the Governor. "Certain steps have been taken that cannot be undone. The marines have men under arrest who will talk, and they've been asked to hand them over to the Navy for safe keeping. Given the general antipathy towards the Watch Company, they'll be happy to do that. So it is going to be difficult to avoid a trial. If these men go on trial, they will inevitably name 'good old uncle Doran.' At that point, not putting him on trial will look like a cover-up, and that will be even worse."

The Governor stood up and walked across to the easel. He studied the painting for a while, and then went and stared out of the window.

"There are too many dead to ignore this time."

Haldar and Willon stood in silence.

The Governor walked back towards them before speaking again. His voice was quieter.

"So what do we do? Bringing him to court would be a political nightmare. The autonomous communities would use it to force political concessions, and it's hard enough getting them to pay their dues as it is. But leaving him unpunished would be a bad message to send out to all the other hangers on." There was a long pause.

Haldar broke it. "I've thought this one through as well; do you want him dead?"

The pause continued and the Governor walked back to the window. As he stood gazing out, Willon could see the man was chewing his lower lip.

"I don't want him unofficially executed or murdered here. If we cannot do it according to the law, I'm not willing to do it. That way leads to the slippery slope I've been trying to keep off since I inherited this job. But he has to be punished in a way that sends out a warning to any others who might be tempted to follow in his footprints."

"What about off-world?"

The Governor stared long and hard at Haldar, "You and that little department of yours have given this a lot of thought. My father always said he didn't need a conscience when he employed you. You seem to have already closed down my easy options. So what have you in mind?"

"Off-world, he is not your responsibility, sir. If he has enemies there and they take their chance at revenge, it is hardly your fault."

"Will he go off-world?"

"He might if you give him a job which appears to be temporary exile as his punishment."

"I will arrange the temporary exile; you deal with the rest of it. We will have a meeting with him." The Governor was decisive. Then he turned to Willon and his voice became less formal. "And are you another of Haldar's conscripts?"

Willon half smiled. "I think so, sir."

"Well, thank you for your assistance, and make sure he pays you cash, it takes months to get a credit note honoured. Last time I heard the details, they were trying to get recipients to set them against moving vehicle offences." With that he ushered them out.

Haldar led Willon down to the gardens.

"I thought I'd better get you to a public area before abandoning you," Haldar said as he brought his wallet out of his pocket. He fished out a number of large denomination notes, folded them and thrust them into Willon's tunic pocket. "If you get bored, you've got my number. Give me a call."

"Will I ever find out what happens to Doran Stilan?"

Haldar smiled as he put his wallet back into his pocket. "You're a journalist; you'll probably find out before me."

Willon noticed that the smile seemed to contain real warmth. Then Haldar continued. "But I'll drop you a note in case you miss it."

He held out his hand, and Willon took it. Then Willon walked across the garden towards the bridge to the rest of the city.

*****

It was late. Outside the windows it was dark. In the Governor's suite the easel had been removed and the Governor sat behind his desk, not on it. Haldar stood to one side, ramrod stiff in his full dress uniform. Vladimir

Kaunas, also in full dress uniform, sat behind his desk, fiddling with his white gloves. The door opened and Doran Stilan entered briskly. There were no guards, no prisoner and escort, no witnesses.

Doran executed a formal salute and stood to attention. "You wished to speak with me, Governor?"

Vladimir gestured at a dossier on the desk by him. "There are questions to answer. Too many questions."

Doran stood in silence. Vladimir continued, "Well,. Have you anything to say in your defence?"

A brief half smile crossed Doran's face. "No sir. Other than perhaps 'Sorry', which I realise is too little and too late."

Haldar found himself staring. In spite of everything, he felt some respect for the guilty man. Even more, he felt a respect for the man's charisma.

Vladimir slammed his hand down on the dossier with a bang and Haldar was sure he saw pain in Doran's eyes. "There are too many people dead here, Doran. Far too many."

Doran responded formally. "I admit my guilt, Governor, I have my letter of resignation on me, and my pistol is unloaded. I will not resist arrest."

"Sod that, Doran. Can you imagine the political ramifications?" The Governor's voice has harsh, strained. "No, you cannot go on trial. Others maybe, but even there, news of your actions could destroy the family and everything we have ever done."

There was silence. Doran's voice was soft. "If Haldar could lend me one round for my pistol, I could solve your problems."

"No." Vladimir almost shouted. "That will just start the gossips and it will be assumed that I had you assassinated. No, you are to go into exile. Find some conference somewhere and you'll go as my ambassador."

"What about my wife and children?"

There was a long silence. "Your wife must make up her own mind. The children can stay here; they're too young to be cast out, any shame should not be theirs."

"And my officers?"

"Haldar?"

Haldar thought furiously. "Some resisted arrest. The Marines have a few survivors. Most of the other ranks surrendered."

"Not all can be considered guilty. I would not like them to suffer, if I am seen to get off scot free."

"They are already being questioned," Haldar said quietly.

"I can give you names, discharge those I name, allow the others to stay in the services, if they want. I picked good men, it would be a pity if the services were to lose them."

"Haldar?" Vladimir looked hard at Haldar. "Well, what do you say?"

"It would avoid a trial; it might even be that most of the guilty are already dead. This one is your decision, I'm afraid, but I will not query it."

"Well, there's a first time for everything." Vladimir sounded like a man who has come to a decision. "Give Haldar the names; they will be off planet and gone within the week. If they come back, they'll face charges. The others will be given the option. As for you, you have two months to settle your affairs, and then go off-world to some appropriate event. Once there, you will remain away for a considerable number of years, during which you will manage to appear busy, and perhaps we might be able to call you back."

Doran snapped to attention and saluted. "Yes Governor."

"Dismissed."

Doran turned smartly and left the room. The Governor sagged in his chair, Haldar remained unmoving. Vladimir turned to him. "Deal with it Haldar. Just make sure I don't have to meet him again until he leaves."

*****

It was three months later; Willon got a note from Haldar, and attached to it a news clipping taken from an out-of-system press agency. Willon read the note with interest.

It appeared that there had been serious breach of security at Finholme Orbital Station. A party from Tsarina, led by Doran Stilan, the Ambassador Plenipotentiary to the 'Salid Sector Conference on the Preservation of Art and Indigenous Culture', had been transferring between ships at the orbital station, and the Ambassador and his wife had been kidnapped. Investigations revealed that one of the merchant ships docked at the station was in reality a Starmancer ship, rumoured to be in the fleet of the notorious Wayland Strang. The clipping finished with a quote from a 'Tsarina Government Source' who stated categorically that the existing policy of not negotiating with pirates and kidnappers would be adhered to, and that no ransom would be paid.

Willon dropped the clipping onto his desk and sat thoughtfully for a while. Then he reviewed his schedule. Tomorrow he had the interview with the six-times winner of the Kaunas City Cribbage Championship. The next two afternoons were the magistrate's court and he had to fit in a visit to the annual garden walk.

He pulled out the paper with Haldar's number, picked up the phone and started to dial.

*****

Out-system Volunteer Rating Taran stood braced in the airlock. One of the other ratings was cycling the air out and Taran ran through the manual checks, tapping the gloved fingers of his left hand on the back of his right hand as a way of ticking them off. The other three members of the customs boarding party stood waiting. The outer door opened and Taran could see the well patched hull of a freighter wallowing next to them.

At the officer's signal, the crewman swung a line thrower away from the wall and cocked it. The crewman checked to see that the line was running free and that none of the boarding party was in the way. Taking careful aim, he fired. The line carrying bolt flew towards the freighter and the magnetic bolt hit three feet from the airlock forward of the upper sponson.

Taran noticed something flashing on his head-up display. He focused on it and it moved to centre field. It was his bank account. It had just been credited with six thousand Thalian Credits.

The lieutenant clipped himself to the line and the rest of the boarding party followed suit. At the back of the group, Taran clicked onto the line. Another day, another job; when his turn came he kicked off toward the freighter.

*****

The holo faded into darkness. The last image was the guttering flames that were consuming the remains of what had once been Doran Stilan. Haldar stared at where the image had been, unwilling to witness the grief of the man next to him.

He knew Vladimir Kaunas was sitting with his face in his hands; he had been for the last hour. Occasionally Haldar had heard a muffled sob, but the silence was worrying him. If Vladimir had raved, had shouted for his guards to have Haldar hauled away, had called for his senior naval staff, that Haldar could have understood; it would have been cathartic for both of them.

For the last two hours, he and Vladimir had been watching the death of Doran Stilan. When he was handed the holochip by a grim faced Toulis, he realised he had misread the situation. Wayland Strang had to remind his captains that no one crossed him. The loss of the Falling Angel meant that discipline had to be restored.

Doran Stilan had taken a month to die. In the course of this, every artifice of the most skilled professionals had been brought to bear. His wife had been tortured and killed as he was forced to watch with eyes already lacking eyelids. Even as the torturers proceeded with their delicate work, news was brought to him that his children were already on their way to join them. At that point Haldar had left the screening to check that Stilan's children were safe. and to take steps to ensure they remained so.

The whole process had been recorded for posterity in high definition detail, a relentless dispassionate 'voice-over' describing each move and discussing its implications. A full month long holo was also commercially available; the narrator had given the name of a wholesaler who would be happy to supply copies at a competitive price for those who served a clientele with specialist tastes. The two hours long 'recorded highlights' had been issued free to every person within the Wayland Strang organisation. The lesson was there to be learned.

They sat in silence still, the room in darkness. Haldar wondered what was running through Vladimir's mind. As Hereditary Governor, and to some extent tyrant, did he see faint shadows of himself in the actions of the man who had given the orders that this should be done? Could he sense within himself the forces which can lead a man to walk the road that Wayland Strang had taken? Could he empathise with the logic?

Next to him he heard Vladimir stir. "Haldar." There was a pause, a silence as if Vladimir was stunned to hear the sound of his own voice at this time.

"Justice must be done, Haldar. I'm not sure I know what justice is any more, and I'm not sure I would dare face it, but I want it done. Wayland Strang must face justice. See to it."

Haldar stood up as if released. He turned to walk to the door, and then glanced down at the man besides him, who was still sitting, staring into the darkness. Briefly, but gently, he laid a hand on Vladimir's shoulder, and then left the room.

Lightning Source UK Ltd.
Milton Keynes UK
UKOW05f1225280714

235889UK00002B/26/P

9 781908 208231